Voices of Upminster

Voices of Upminster

Cecilia Pyke

Front cover: Walter Knight with Nell Aggiss, *c.* 1890s.
Frontispiece: Corbets Tey Road, 1906.

First published 2008
Reprinted 2014

The History Press Ltd
The Mill, Brimscombe Port
Stroud, Gloucestershire, GL5 2QG
www.thehistorypress.co.uk

© Cecilia Pyke, 2008

The right of Cecilia Pyke to be identified as the Author
of this work has been asserted in accordance with the
Copyrights, Designs and Patents Act 1988.

All rights reserved. No part of this book may be reprinted
or reproduced or utilised in any form or by any electronic,
mechanical or other means, now known or hereafter invented,
including photocopying and recording, or in any information
storage or retrieval system, without the permission in writing
from the Publishers.
British Library Cataloguing in Publication Data.
A catalogue record for this book is available from the British Library.

ISBN 978 0 7524 4556 4

Typesetting and origination by The History Press Ltd.
Printed in Great Britain

Acknowledgements

Every effort has been made to trace the copyright owners of old photographs reproduced in this book. With thanks to the Royal Veterinary College for the photograph taken in the college library, and to the London Borough of Havering Local Studies for the loan of old pictures of Upminster. Thanks also to Upminster Golf Club for providing the copy of the Upminster Hall engraving, and to Roomes for the Eastex display photograph. Finally, thank you to all those who contributed photographs from their private collections – most especially Mr Eric Knight for allowing me to use the wonderful family photograph for the cover of this book.

References:

Victoria County History of Essex
Our Old Upminster and District by Ted Ballard

Contents

	INTRODUCTION	9
ONE	EARLY LIFE	13
TWO	SCHOOLDAYS	21
THREE	SHOPS	33
FOUR	WAR YEARS	41
FIVE	BUSINESSES AND SERVICES	47
SIX	FARMLANDS	59
SEVEN	PLACES OF INTEREST	73
EIGHT	PROFESSIONS	95
NINE	ENTERTAINERS	107
TEN	REFLECTIONS	115

Introduction

Upminster has existed as a community since the Romans took over its fertile farmlands as long ago as 500 BC. Agriculture has always been important to the area and, even now, we are surrounded by fields even if fewer crops are produced.

The history of Upminster has already been well recorded, so within these pages we deal mostly with its more recent past from the perspective of some of the people who have lived and worked here, as they speak with their own 'voice'.

In the last 100 years, the town, as with all London suburbs, has grown immeasurably. By necessity its character has altered and will continue to change as the population of London explodes, and more accommodation is provided in surrounding areas.

Within the limitations of one book it is impossible to cover every aspect of a community, but those who were born in the first quarter of the last century remember Upminster as a village and are justly proud of their roots.

Ted Ballard, in his book *Our Old Upminster and District*, records that stocks were still in place in 1814 and the village pond existed in about 1851.

Walking along Corbets Tey Road now, it is difficult to imagine that it was once a country lane flanked by grand houses, built mostly in the 1700s. These were sold off and pulled down by developers in the 1920s and 1930s to create the estates on the town's southern side.

Most of the houses in Hall Lane were owned by rich businessmen whose children were able to play outside, disturbed only by the occasional horse-drawn vehicle.

Gas supplies arrived in about 1880 and the main sewage system was laid in 1899 although many houses still were not connected until the 1920s. 1885 brought the steam railway, with the South Ockendon Branch Line opening in 1892, and the Romford line in 1893. Before then, businessmen who lived in Upminster and further afield were wealthy and led privileged lives. They would have gone to Romford Station by private carriage and then by train to their offices in London.

The excitement of the hunt is remembered when it met in the centre of Upminster before making its way to the Huntsman and Hounds in Corbets Tey. Picture the hunt meeting on a misty morning and the clatter of hoofs as riders assembled in the village centre. Imagine the riders in their red jackets with the hounds barking – all waiting for the call of the horn. How exciting for the village children to experience this spectacle, now relegated to the past. It is unimaginable now that Corbets Tey once had a larger population than Upminster village.

Perhaps the most profound changes began in 1932 when the District Line was extended from Barking to Upminster. This made access to London and West End offices easier, and brought workers looking for somewhere pleasant to live with their families. With the truly wealthy now gone, their old estates were developed into leafy avenues of houses. Expansion of housing brought more shops, together with the infrastructure required to sustain a growing population.

The village green was replaced by The Broadway and became what we now know as Bell Corner, where once the Bell Hotel stood – another landmark pulled down in the name of progress. The 1950s brought more change when the Cosy Corner Café – so fondly remembered – was demolished in order that the roads could be widened and traffic lights installed at Bell Corner.

Oral history is now accepted as a vital resource for learning about the past and how people lived – without it, our history is less colourful and we lose the essence of how communities functioned. As they tell their stories we learn a little of the lives of 'ordinary' people as well as those in professions, while along the way we uncover some interesting facts.

Blacksmith James Leech, Corbets Tey, *c.* 1800s.

The Windmill, 2008.

Upminster's past is also uncovered by contributors bringing to life the fascinating history of some of its buildings. The mind can wander to the old hunting lodge and infirmary which preceded Upminster Hall. It is easy to imagine the hooded monks going about their daily tasks.

Much has been written about the windmill, but our interest is captured as we learn how it functioned as a business and as ownership changed. We are united with the aspirations for its future.

Memory is acknowledged to be subjective, so if perhaps the reader remembers differently, so be it and I apologise for any errors or omissions.

My thanks go to all the people who gave their time so generously and loaned photographs in order that this book could be produced. I was welcomed by gracious people whom I think of with warmth and gratitude.

one

Early Life

Cod Liver Oil and Sardines

My family lived on the Upminster Park estate and, as a child, I was given cod-liver oil and concentrated orange juice which I loved, but you never see it now. All the mothers were rather afraid of the health visitor; mine had arguments with hers about my bottle feeding, as my mother felt I was not drinking enough. And yet, because I was premature, there was a risk in giving me too much milk. I remember going to the clinic, but compared with Dr Wallace's surgery, it seemed rather run down.

Many middle-class people were poor in the 1950s but learned to budget carefully by preparing simple meals and doing repairs instead of replacing items. They made things themselves out of wooden orange boxes and the like. I remember when I was very small my mother opened a can of sardines and placed one sardine each on some fingers of toast. She put them on a plate in the sitting room and was horrified when, a few minutes later, she discovered I'd eaten all of them when they'd been intended as the evening meal for the three of us. Just before my first Christmas in 1956 my mother bought some Danish Blue cheese and bacon, and stored it in my pram. When she came out of the next shop she discovered I'd eaten the cheese and chewed the bacon. She began to cry as it was all she could afford for Christmas.

My dentist was in Station Road. He was easily irritated and not very pleasant to his patients. For some reason he didn't give men an anæsthetic, although he gave one to women. I remember very vividly having a root canal without anaesthetic, on a decayed tooth when I was about thirteen. It was so painful he could only drill for two or three seconds at a time so this tried his patience, despite holding my head in an armlock.

I don't recall playing organised games very much but boys played tag in the playground and girls played hopscotch and skipped with a rope. There were always grids chalked on the pavements in Avon Road and there were so few cars that children were able to play in the roads. Only one family in our road had a car and the owner was a salesman. When I was seven I was knocked down by one of the few cars on the estate and broke my leg. The car belonged to the Baptist minister.

We had more freedom to roam in those days and I often amused myself in the playing fields and woods which are next to the tithe barn. The upper half of the playing fields were still sown with barley and the annual burning of the stubble was a major event, with fire engines always present – probably as a precautionary measure.

When I was about eight, my mother gave me a 10s note to buy something for her at the shops. I came back minus the money and without what I'd been sent out to buy. I was unable to offer an explanation of what had happened to the money, and my mother and I walked up and down Avon Road asking people if they had seen the 10s note. We didn't find it and my mother was quite upset as it was a big part of her house-keeping budget.

The police station in Upminster was open at all hours and a bobby was usually on the beat on the estate. Perhaps even more importantly, the men of the estate would have soon put a stop to any teenage misbehaviour before it became serious, but the need never arose. Most of us were terrified of getting into trouble with our parents – I was much more worried about my parents than my teachers if I did anything wrong.

There were characteristic smells which wafted over the estate from time to time. One was the smell of malting barley from the Ind Coope Brewery in Romford and the other was a smell of chemicals from the May & Baker works in Dagenham. The former was quite common when there was malting going on but we usually only smelled the latter when the wind was in the right direction, as the plant was about four miles away as the crow flies.

We had a holiday in the UK every year, usually in Scotland because my mother was Scottish, but we also went to Swanage and north Wales. In 1962 my father bought his first car, which was an Austin A40, and so from 1963 onwards we were able to take motoring holidays abroad. My father frequently worked in Italy so we went there with him in 1966.

The GPs needed for the new estate were placed in large detached houses with adjoining surgeries rather than in clinics. This worked well initially but had an inherent problem in that the houses belonged to the GPs personally and not to the NHS. By far the most popular GP was Dr John Anthony in Cranham, but his list was very full.

Our GP was Dr Wallace who had his surgery at the junction of Avon Road and Severn Drive, opposite the Golden Crane. He was Scottish and really put himself out for his patients, making home visits and even breaking off from gardening one day to vaccinate me. Sadly, he decided to go to North America in the mid-1960s but I think he came back to Upminster and opened a practice on the south side of town.

I was brought up in the period when the NHS was trying to improve the health of children. I had all the available vaccinations, including smallpox and polio, but this was before the MMR vaccine and I contracted measles, mumps and rubella during my childhood.

Peter Morris

Early Life

Golden Crane, Upminster Park Estate.

The Alley

My parents brought me to Upminster in 1923 when I was three months old. I used to walk along Corbets Tey Road with my mother when it was a country lane, and can recall some of the big houses down there – Londons, West Lodge, and Hunts Hall farmhouse, etc. Some eighty years ago Hall Lane was also a long country lane, so I've seen Upminster grow from a sleepy village to a prosperous little town. Our cottage was in St Mary's Lane and opposite St Laurence Church. We lived in The Alley, but in those days the locals referred to it as 'up the alley'.

We had no water laid on so all the cottages drew water from the communal tap which was at the front. The toilet was across the backyard and was one of those bucket-type things that had to be emptied every so often. Our cottage was at the end of the row and adjacent to Abraham's windmill. As children, Mr Abraham would pick us up and lift us over the fence so we could run across the field to the mill. He used his own milled flour in the little baker's shop he had just around the corner.

My father sent us to a Sunday school held by the Band of Hope, which is a temperance society. It was formed in Leeds in 1847 to teach working-class children the evils of drink, and

Corbets Tey Road, c. 1900.

its members took a vow of abstinence. The Sunday school was held in the Congregational church, and I recall the Pudney boys were members too.

I'm not sure why we left the cottage near the mill – I think it might have been pulled down, as we moved into Garbutt Road. After that we went to live in Cranham Cottage which was between the Thatched House and the Jobbers Rest.

Bess Anglin

Roomes Stores

Since there was a war on when I was a child, there wasn't too much to do in Upminster, so my life seems to have revolved around walking and shopping. Mum would send me to

Early Life

Hall Lane, *c.* 1890.

the shops and I'd loiter looking in all the windows. Roomes had glass showcases outside at that time and we children used to chase around them, playing hide-and-seek. The floor manager, Mr Timms, would come out to tell us off, but we thought it great fun. Besides there being a restaurant on the top floor, Roomes also had a little shop selling cakes and pastries which had been freshly baked in the restaurant. Often, as a treat, my mother would send me there for half a dozen of their delicious raspberry buns.

We also used to frequent the Thistle Café which was on the left-hand side at the top of Howard Road.

Maggie Ollington

Boys will be boys

My parents came to live in Upminster in 1936 when my father, who was an industrial chemist, took a position with May & Baker. Both my father and mother came from naval families and I was born in Gosport, Hampshire, in 1944. Since the dockyard was so heavily fortified and out of range of the V2s, it was thought safer for my mother to give birth in Gosport, and we didn't come back to Upminster until I was three months old.

As boys, we made our own fun. In those days (the 1950s) we used to go into the Furze fields at the bottom of Park Drive because we enjoyed building a dam in a stream that ran through there. We'd wait until the water built up to about 2ft and then break the dam – the water would come out with a 'whoosh' and we'd have great fun. During the war a V2 had landed in the field behind the houses in Argyle Gardens between the end of Park Drive and Springfield Gardens. A pond had formed in the crater and we'd make our own little boats to sail on it. It could only have been about 2ft deep because we could walk in it with our wellies on. We made camps in what we called the forest which was a bit further round. We'd also pretend to smoke by crushing dock seeds – when they dried they looked like tobacco. One puff was enough, as it tasted foul. Perhaps that's why to this day I don't smoke!

When we'd finished our homework my friend and I would often go over to the fields to fly our control-line model aircraft. The engines ran on diesel fuel which we mixed ourselves with paraffin, castor oil and ether – we worked out they reached a speed of 68mph. We built the planes from plans we bought from *Aero Modeller* magazine. I finally built a model of a Spitfire, which I still have, with its ED racer engine still in it.

Richard Moorey

The Bell Hotel

People were more open in the 1940–50s and didn't lock their back doors. We didn't have a television when I was small, and on one occasion I let myself into a friend's house when the family was out. They returned home and found me sitting in an armchair, large as life, watching their television. Years later the daughter of that family recalled coming to our house because she knew mum would give her an orange. They didn't have oranges in her house, although they had television.

The Bell Hotel had old-fashioned Georgian windows and we'd press our noses against them as we watched the people dancing in the function rooms. They were at the rear of the hotel and were used for weddings and dances, etc. I remember seeing wicker furniture in there. We'd try to buy a beer in the public bar at the end, just for a lark, but were always refused.

My friend's mother treasured a carrier bag that cost her 3d and one day we borrowed it to gather conkers in the fields near Cranham Church. On the way we passed a garden in which peaches were growing, so we decided to have them instead. We were just about to start picking them when the owner shouted at us, so we ran away leaving the bag behind. That was another telling off we got from his mum when we got home. It was only a paper

Early Life

The Bell Hotel, *c.* 1905.

carrier bag and it's hard to think it was precious in those days, compared to nowadays when we throw plastic bags away all the time.

The shops at the end of Argyle Gardens were built on an old pond and there were no flood drains for when it rained heavily. The ground floor of the confectionary shop flooded regularly until the council put in proper drainage. The owners would put their chairs on the table because they could expect the water to rise about 6in. We boys would have great fun sitting on the pavement with our feet dangling in the water. We'd eagerly wait for cars to come by which would create a big wave but, unfortunately for us, there wasn't much traffic about then. Next door to the Masons Arms there was an alleyway where we used to explore the derelict and bombed buildings – they've since built bungalows on the site. When I grew older we'd play roller-skating hockey in Howard Road because it had a dead end before they built the new houses along there. We'd play football on Cranham cricket ground pitch for hours on end and get another telling off for not coming home on time. There was a place we called Creeper Wood because you could cut the creeper and smoke it. We amused ourselves by building camps and tracking.

One Sunday in each month my dad used to take me for a bike ride through the lanes to Rainham. We'd visit a friend of his in Parsonage Road, and cycling around the lanes made a nice trip out.

There were two semi-detached cottages in St Mary's Lane before the petrol station was built along by the Masons Arms. The cottages have since been replaced by six detached houses and next door is a house made of red brick. An old lady used to live there and she'd wait in St Mary's Lane with her empty beer bottles to ask somebody to go to the off-licence to buy her some brown ale. Whoever bought the ale kept the money that was due back on the empty bottles, so we loved going into the Masons to buy it for her. We were only about seven – imagine going into an off-licence underage nowadays!

Alex Duffey

two

Schooldays

Carpentry

I lived and went to school in Rainham. At the back of the school was a small building where the cookery and carpentry classes were held. At some point the building was taken over entirely by the cookery class so they had to find somewhere else for the carpentry group to go. I was about thirteen at the time, so this was in the 1930s, and it was decided we'd go to a class held in the hall at the back of Trinity Church, close to Roomes in Upminster.

We were taken from Rainham by bus to Upminster every Friday afternoon for about two years. There were about twenty of us boys, and the bus was an American Chevrolet with a platform on the back. Naturally we all fought to stand on the platform for the journey.

Initially we learned how to make joints – tenon, mortise and dovetail – and then went on to make things. I can remember making a tea-pot stand out of oak which had fancy engravings on it, and another thing was a stand for a pocket watch. I wish now I had kept some of the things I made. We all had a wonderful time at those lessons, before the bus came to take us home at four o'clock.

Charlie Bifield

Miss Bush and Mr Lacey

Initially the younger children on the Upminster Park estate had gone to the infants' school in Upminster, popularly known as The Bell School, but Engayne School was built on the estate in 1958. From the age of about three, I went to a nursery twice a week for a couple of hours in the Masonic Hall in Deyncourt Gardens. I think I joined the infants' school at Engayne in Easter 1961, when I was just five. Miss Bush was the headmistress and she was always very good to me. The original annexe was built in the playground around 1963 and, later, another was built in Marlborough Gardens. The headmaster of the whole school, and specifically the middle school, was Mr Lacey. He was an excellent, if stern, headmaster of the 'old school' who ran a tight ship. I think he deserves the credit for the lack of unruly children on the estate in its early days. Many of his pupils went on to university at a time when it was usual for only 10 per cent of the population to do so. Hardly any of the parents had gone to university but many had gained qualifications at night school. The (then uncovered) swimming pool was built just before I left the school in 1967.

I remember having to take in money to school to buy stamps for my National Savings card and the daily milk ration. I also recall raising money for Aberfan after the disaster there. We were all horrified at what had happened but I always felt raising money was pretty pointless, and so it proved. Most of my teachers were nice and good at their job.

Peter Morris

Convent Grounds

I have fond memories of the huge grounds at the back of the convent when I went to school there in the 1960s. One field was laid to lawn and planted with large circles of rhododendron bushes. They were a magnificent sight in the summer when the huge flowers were in bloom – the whole area was a blaze of pink blossom. Sometimes in summer the nuns would open the French doors and sit out and have tea on the lawn. We had to walk past one field to get to another where hockey matches and games of rounders were played. Sports events were held there as well. If the weather was bad then sometimes we'd play rounders in the hall.

We were forbidden to go into the large orchard which was at the side of the school building but, naturally, we couldn't resist scrumping. On one particular day I climbed a tree and was quite happily throwing apples down to my friends below, when there was a loud clap. My name was called and I was told in no uncertain terms to climb down and leave the orchard immediately. I looked up to see the art teacher looking down on me from the art classroom window. Later, when I saw her in school, she threatened to report me to the head teacher if she caught me in the orchard again.

Just past the orchard and hidden from view there was a large pond. When the science teacher wanted some worms to dissect during a lesson, my friend and I volunteered to gather some from the pond, making sure we kept the fattest ones for ourselves. When it was time to go home for the day, there was always a nun at the door to check we were wearing our hats and that belts were buckled up. It was impressed upon us that when we were in uniform our behaviour reflected on the school.

Colleen Mallon

The School Bus and Sports

When I was in the juniors I used to catch a school bus just outside the farm gate. Sometimes I'd stand there with my mother until ten or eleven o'clock waiting for it to turn up. Sometimes it didn't arrive because it couldn't get through the roads which had been bombed, and at other times it didn't bother to come when it was foggy. So, my early education was neglected because I was hardly ever at school. I lagged well behind those who lived close to the school because another factor was the lack of teachers – the young men were away fighting which also meant we played no sports.

Also when I was in the juniors, we'd go over to Abraham's the bakers and buy a penny bun – I'm sure the shop was there up until the fifties. I didn't learn much until I went to Gaynes School and began to play cricket. Once at Gaynes my life changed and I couldn't wait to get there every day. We were streamed in those days and I began in Form 1C and finished in 4A. When I took my last exam I came sixth in the class, and it was entirely due to my interest in sport that I never wanted to miss school.

I loved cricket and my first match was played against Drury Falls. I played for two years on the intermediate side, then for two years on the senior side. For the last year on the senior side, I was captain of Gaynes and represented the school when we played against Romford and district schools. The Upminster football pitch was where the swings are now. The Hornchurch football team evolved from the old Upminster team – it became Upminster & Hornchurch, then just Hornchurch. The cricket pitch is still in the same place. The football team changed their clothes in what used to be the British Legion hut, which was where the library is now.

Bert Bonnett

St Joseph's

Each year in May I took part in the annual procession to the convent from St Joseph's Church in Champion Road. The convent grounds were absolutely beautiful – there were three little altars in the gardens which we'd visit as we made our way round. The girls wore their white first-communion dresses.

Procession for the first communion, 1960s.

My brothers and sister went by bus to St Mary's School in the Hornchurch Road. In the 1940s our priest, Father McKenna, decided he'd like to set up a primary Catholic school in Upminster. The Sacred Heart was fee paying at the time, so he asked the local Catholic families if they'd send their children to his new school if he was able to provide one. He had no money to pay for it, no building, no official backing, nothing. This meant transferring children from St Mary's in Hornchurch, but my parents decided to leave my elder sister there. She was about ten at that time so would be leaving soon anyway, but they said that both my brother, Richard, and I could go to the new school. Richard was about seven and, although I was only three, I was sent there to make the numbers up.

Denis, who's since died, had been sent to the Sacred Heart when he was about four, but asked to be taken away because there were too many girls. Mum pushed me to the new school in the pushchair on the first day but because I cried they let me have a few days off, and after that my brother had to look after me.

There was no school building so classes were held in a large hall where the presbytery has since been built. We were sectioned off by wooden screens built by Mr Main, who was one of the fathers. Later we used the room under the church where the youth club meets now, and the priests' house which at that time was where the junior classrooms now border the playground. There were only a few qualified teachers to begin with and no money to provide school dinners, but somebody in the parish supplied the food, and mothers came in on a voluntary basis to cook it. One lad had to go round the back of one of the buildings to get the coal out from under the church and bring it round to stoke the boiler so we had some heating.

Sister Agatha from the Sacred Heart Convent was our first headmistress and she alone would know what difficulties she had to cope with. I remember her as being very small in stature but quite strict – she certainly threatened the boys with the cane, but she was also very kind. People didn't have much spare cash in those days so fund-raising efforts must have been strenuous, because the school survived and grew, and recently celebrated its fiftieth anniversary.

I stayed at St Josephs until I was eleven, when I went to the St Ursuline Convent in Brentwood on the school coach. Somehow I'd managed to pass the eleven-plus which had been brought in by then. If you passed you went to the Ursuline, and if not, to the Sacred Heart, which by this time was no longer fee paying.

Pat Duffey

Romford College

When I was old enough I started at the school where Barclays Bank has since been built, and later went to The Bell School when it opened. There was a church school where Westminster Bank is now – I remember it had a spire which was taken off at a later date. After that I went to Romford College which was a private school in Victoria Road. I never wanted to do anything else but become a farmer and began work on the farm as soon as I left school.

Eric Knight

Minster House and Palmer's College

When I was about four, I began attending Minster House which was a little private school run by Mr and Mrs Hartley. For the first year we were taught by a lovely lady called Miss Headley and I was very disappointed when I had to go up to the next year. I also recall Mr Dobson, who taught there for many years, and a Mr Harris and the Revd Breaze. During the war Minster House was requisitioned by the authorities, so the school moved into Stranraer, which is a house on the corner of Parklands Avenue and Corbets Tey Road. Stranraer was later owned by Mr Wylie, the vet. The school had moved back to Minster House when I started there in the late forties and I think it closed shortly after Mr and Mrs Hartley retired.

Minster House School, which was originally called Hill House School, was almost opposite the windmill in St Mary's Lane, and most children seemed to stay until the age of about thirteen. The house has since been demolished and replaced by a more modern one.

When I was old enough to go to senior school I went to Palmer's in Grays. At first I went on the No.370 bus and then realised most of my friends were going by train. The steam trains had just finished and were replaced by diesel units. Before the diesel engines took over, some boys would go from carriage to carriage while the train was moving – you could lower the window by the leather strap, open the door and walk along the running board. The line was on a single track, and before electronic signalling and points came in we'd watch the drivers exchange keys for the points. The driver needed to make sure there was only one train on the track so he'd have a big brass ring with a sort of key on it. He'd lean out of the window and the signalman would take the key from him and open the points with it. The driver of the next train back would take the key down to the other end and this meant two trains could share the track. We loved to get seats near the driver to watch him pass the key to the signalman, and a huge roar went up if he dropped it! Trains with diesel units weren't so much fun.

Richard Moorey

Deyncourt Gardens

Until I was old enough to go to senior school, I went to a little private school at the end of Deyncourt Gardens called Upminster College. Miss Curry was the headmistress and classes were held in a little prefabricated building that consisted of just three rooms, with the toilets on a veranda outside. Although the building wasn't much, the education was very good. As juniors, we were taught such subjects as simple French, mathematics and algebra.

I went to the convent in Upminster when I was about eleven. At that time the nuns wore a very strict habit with the long navy-blue skirt and veil. Although our schooling was strict we were very happy as the nuns were wonderful to us. I loved them all so much I went back to the convent to teach when I got my art qualifications, and stayed there for thirty-five years.

Maggie Ollington

The Sacred Heart of Mary Convent

When I was at The Bell School I took my eleven-plus and failed, so my parents applied for me to go the convent, which in 1946 cost seven guineas per term, with music and dancing

Maggie Ollington in her convent school days, second from the right.

lessons etc. costing extra. Our school books were supplied by the little St Mary's Library at 162 St Mary's Lane, which later became a china shop, but it's gone now.

In 1948 the King and Queen passed through Upminster on their way to Tilbury – I think it was in connection with their Silver Wedding celebrations. We convent schoolchildren were really excited as we lined St Mary's Lane, and Sister Alcantra was very strict about us keeping our toes exactly on the kerb edge – woe betide any girl whose foot strayed. I remember being disappointed when the Queen looked over at the windmill instead of noticing us. We used to call a lot of the land that's now known as Upminster Park, 'the rec'. It was originally owned by St Laurence Church before they relinquished it for public use. Our school uniform colours were pale and navy blue. In winter our basic uniform was all navy blue, with the dress having a cream Peter Pan collar, and cream gym blouses. We wore a distinctive blue and navy-striped blazer, and I loved mine so much I still have it. In summer we wore a blue-striped cotton dress with a Panama hat. The colour for the boys' uniform differed slightly in that their trousers and pullover were grey.

Voices of Upminster

Convent school fees, 1947.

I was in the school choir and Mother Austin liked us to look smart so would rearrange the order that Mr Heywood, the choirmaster, had put us in. This would infuriate him as he had us in sections for different voices. Sister Dot liked cats and would encourage them to come and eat, so we seemed to have hundreds of them hanging around.

When it first opened, the school was very small, so the pupils were taught in the private house, but a new school building was built alongside and officially opened in May 1930. It took children from all denominations with girls of all ages from five to sixteen, and boys up to the age of eight. At that time there was a small number of boarders. Then a new wing was added and a red-brick chapel was built as well. It was ready for worship in 1935, but had to be pulled down in the 1960s as it began to subside. Because of this, a chapel was created in one of the rooms in the convent and sometimes this was used by pupils, but big masses were held in the main school hall. The school had never asked for public assistance, and was funded entirely by the Religious of the Sacred Heart of Mary. Every Saturday morning the boarders had riding lessons at Frank's Riding School which was at the farm in St Mary's Lane, and some pupils were sent to 'finishing school' in Paris or Rome. As more pupils wanted to go to the school, the buildings had to be enlarged and they were in the middle of a programme when the Second World War was declared.

Because the convent was so close to London, and more especially Hornchurch aerodrome, it was thought best to find a safer place for the children. So, a lease was taken on Chilton House in Buckinghamshire and the school was evacuated, but some of the sisters stayed and continued to teach at St Mary's.

Chilton House was owned by Sir Henry Aubrey-Fletcher, who lived with his family on the home farm. He seems to have been a very nice man, as on their first morning he invited the six sisters who had organised the move to have breakfast with his family. So the old house and school buildings in Upminster were more or less empty, with just a few sisters living there. But soon it was requisitioned by the Army, with troops being billeted in the school and officers living in the convent. Because of this, the sisters still living there had to find other accommodation, so they moved into a house in Boundary Road, but they were able to take a break from the bombing by making trips to Chilton House. During the war, the old coach house and some outhouses were demolished by a bomb but no major damage was done to the house.

The school came back from Buckinghamshire when the war ended and reopened in September 1946. At that time, it received so many applications from new pupils that another programme of building was begun to provide more accommodation for boarders. In 1950 the school became a secondary modern school for Catholic girls and it changed to voluntary-aided status. The boarders were sent to a convent in Hillingdon in Middlesex to finish their education and within five years the school was completely Catholic. In 1978 the school changed its status again to become comprehensive and more extensions were added as the intake got bigger yet again. In 1983 it handed over to lay management.

Convent of the Sacred Heart of Mary.

When I began working at the Sacred Heart as school secretary in 1974 there were around 464 pupils, and now there are over 800.

Val Eland

Miss Kylick

When I went to The Bell School, Miss Kylick used to be one of the music mistresses. She had a black stick with a green tip on the end, which she used to point out the notes to us. Her appearance was quite severe as she arranged her hair in two buns on her ears. She'd also be on the stage in the dinner hall while we were eating. If we took back a plate which still had food on it, she'd send us back to the table to finish our food.

The cane was used in my school days – I think just on the hand – and I remember one boy ran home when it was his turn. We had country dancing in 'the quad' and our parents would come to watch us. There was an annexe to the school, near to where the latest Roomes building is, just where the petrol station used to be, and we had some classes in there. For some reason, our sports' master used to sleep in the building. For a couple of years he coached us for cricket in the Easter holidays and football in the summer, with the result that we won the cups for both cricket and football in the third and fourth years.

I went to Gaynes School until 1960 where I took part in sports and other activities, so thoroughly enjoyed my time there. We had two gardening lessons a week and wore special boots when we did something called double-digging. There was a brook at the end of the gardens and we went for walks over Cranham marshes, and took part in cross-country running.

Alex Duffey

Always the First

I went to the infants' school when it first opened in St Mary's Lane, and when the time came for me to go to senior school Gaynes had just been opened, so I was one of the first pupils to go there too.

Bess Anglin

three

Shops

Argyle Gardens

As a child I lived in Argyle Gardens, so we used the shops at the St Mary's Lane end of the road. There were three shops in the little parade – there was Grummitt's on the corner, which was the newsagents, then Barry Patchett's uncle had the middle shop which was a deli. His dad had the end one which sold fruit and veg. The foundations for a row of six shops had been laid at that time, but initially only three were built. Later the remaining three were put up, and Barry Hurst's father opened one as a cobbler's. We used the grocer's which was just by the Masons Arms. My Dad worked for Fords and if he was out on strike – and sometimes he'd be out for three months at a time – the little grocer's would put the bill on the slate.

I remember Pearks' as being a shop I liked because we were able to get broken biscuits in there. Pearks' was opposite Rivett's in St Mary's Lane.

Alex Duffey

Tesco

In the 1950s, there was a very small Tesco at the end of Corbets Tey Road. It was a funny little shop that used to display its wares outside, and this was frowned upon. It seemed to be all right for greengrocers to have their vegetables outside the shop, but not others.

Val Eland

Grandfather's Fish Shop

My grandfather was one of the earlier residents in Upminster in the 1920s – he'd lived there before I was born. He had a fish shop opposite the Capitol Cinema in St Mary's Lane, where Somerfield now stands. On the right-hand side going towards Cranham was Gidden's wood yard, then Tudor Gardens and then the cinema. It wasn't terribly large, and almost opposite was Grandfather's fish shop.

When I was a child, little green waste bins were attached to lampposts and people could advertise their services on them. My grandfather used to do this and our advert read, 'A is for Anglin and Anglin for Fish'. He sold wet fish but in later years did fried fish as well. Granddad was quite a prominent man in Upminster – I recall he also had a business in Billingsgate and Dad used to work for him. They'd get up before four o'clock in the morning to go to the fish market.

Grandfather's name was Thomas Alfred, as was my father's, and he lived in Ivydene which was opposite the clock tower. I seem to recall he lived in one of a row of rather large houses. Eventually Grandfather gave up the fish shop and became a corn and seed merchant, but later sold the business to Cramphorns. When I grew up I worked for him for a while because we were expecting to go to war, and my parents didn't want me to travel to London. I stayed on for a while when Cramphorns took over but eventually went to work for Roomes.

I remember Pudney's – that was the florists near to the railway station where they sold plants and flowers.

Then there was Humphreys, the chemist shop that later on became Storeys. Bonanza was along there – that shop was to become Bon Marché where they sold children's wear. Bonanza was run by an elderly lady who stood in the doorway wearing a long skirt. It was an Aladdin's cave, full of gifts and fancy goods.

Mr Jupps the butcher was just past the Cosy Corner. My parents moved to 127 St Mary's Lane which was one of two houses that were just past Aggiss's garage and The Alley. Then came Green's stores, with its two little steps, and possibly a wool shop, then the two houses which had long front gardens.

At what is now the main crossroads, was The Bell Hotel on one corner, the Cosy Corner Café on another, St Laurence Church on the third, with Aggiss's garage and a few shops on the other corner.

Mr Searson who ran the shoe shop had a bad leg – I can still picture him limping through the shop to serve us. My father always made us wear good shoes so we'd go to Searson's to be fitted for our Startrites.

Bess Anglin

Bell Corner, 1950s.

Fondly Remembered

I was taken to Searson's in Station Road to buy my Startrite shoes. They used an X-ray machine to get a proper fitting and I liked seeing the bones in my feet in ghostly green. The machine was there until the 1970s, although there was a big campaign against them, mainly in the USA. It was led by the chemist Linus Pauling in the 1950s and 1960s but it never reached Upminster.

In the 1950–60s, Woolworths in Corbets Tey Road had sawdust on the floor and I recall the weighing machine with its large round dial. You could buy a slider, which was a block of ice cream, with two wafers, or have your block put into a square cone. If you were celebrating you could buy an 'oyster', which was an ice cream in an oyster-shaped wafer dipped in chocolate at one end and dusted with coconut flakes. I think I only had one of those once.

My mother was very fond of the Co-operative butchers because it always had fresh meat. The Co-operative store was also very popular and often attracted long queues which stretched most of the way round the shop. It did a roaring trade on Ford's paydays as it cashed pay cheques and would give the change in cash. My mother looked forward to her first dividend day and was very disappointed with the meagre payout, saying it would have been much larger in her native Scotland. Eventually the Co-op changed over to blue stamps, which paid a much smaller bonus and, to add to the disappointment, you had to go all the way to East Ham to exchange them for something you chose from a catalogue.

I recall Dobson's in Station Road when it was still an old-fashioned ironmonger's shop with lawnmowers on show. There was a definite smell in Dobson's which disappeared when it became a homeware store. It was a bit like creosoted wood, and I always thought it came from the wooden floor but may have been oil from the lawnmowers and garden tools.

You could leave a list at a local shop, especially the Home and Colonial in Station Road, and your order would be delivered by a boy on a bike. It was run along old-fashioned lines with a formidable husband and wife team working behind a counter. They had their favourites who were served first and they tended to ignore children like me. I remember dry goods such as rice, split peas and dried butterbeans being weighed and put into brown paper bags. The Home and Colonial has long since gone and been replaced by Phoenix Kitchens.

Finlays had a newspaper stall in Upminster Station. It was small yet sold a full range of newspapers, magazines and tobacco. I think there was an even smaller stall near the door which sold sweets. Perhaps it also belonged to Finlays – it sold tobacco as well.

Martins, the newsagent, was also run by a very efficient husband and wife team. I think the husband had been a professional soldier so ran his shop along military lines and came down heavily on the newspaper boy who was late for work or delivered the wrong paper. The sweet counter was on the left-hand side of the shop and made of glass and varnished pine. Loose sweets were kept in drawers with compartments, and we children used to take ages to choose what we wanted to spend our penny on. I bought bubble gum from Martins for the interesting inserts rather than the gum, and in the 1960s there were two interesting series. One was replica Confederate money which seemed highly exotic as I hadn't come across modern American money then, and the other was a series of cards about the American Civil War written from a strongly pro-Confederate point of view – the 'disaster' of Atlanta, etc.

Harvey's the greengrocer's was also popular as they sold a wide variety of excellent vegetables.

I also remember Walters, the stationery shop in Corbets Tey Road, and Peter the Canadian hairdresser in St Mary's Lane.

My mother was very fond of Sainsbury's after it opened in Corbets Tey Road, as it was much better than the bigger Sainsbury's elsewhere. Initially it only had two aisles but later expanded into the shop next door. It was particularly good for cheap ham hocks which my mother used for making soup.

There was a very good tobacco and pipe shop in Corbets Tey Road, next to Walters the stationers – it might have been called Griggs. It had old tobacco jars in its window and was run by a father and his son.

Debenhams bought out Stone's, which was in Romford Market place, and it was in the very last days of the animal market that we bought our dog, in 1962. My parents remembered the cattle and sheep on show in Romford Market in the mid-1950s.

Much of our shopping was delivered. Milk and eggs were delivered by Florrie, the milk lady, who I think had a farm near Grays. The Sunblest bread van came round every morning up to at least 1977. There was also a vegetable van which came less often, and until the early 1970s the onion Johnny came over from Normandy every year with his strings of onions and garlic.

Before the shops opened in Avon Road around 1958, my mother did most of her shopping in the centre of Upminster, pushing my pram there and back. She went 'down the road' every day. Even when just going 'down the road', she would put on a scarf – I remember a yellow wool one with foxes' heads – and white gloves.

Peter Morris

Station Road

Mr Searson owned the shoe shop and I was friendly with Barbara, one of his daughters. I'd go to birthday parties in the flat above the shop, and after we'd had tea Mr Searson would allow us downstairs to play 'shoes'. He must have been very patient as he'd allowed us to pretend we were serving customers and we had a lovely time. He didn't seem to mind us taking shoes out of the boxes to try them on.

Another shop I remember is the tiny one next to Dobson's. It was owned by a Mr Copley who smoked a clay pipe. He had a very bushy moustache and reminded me of something from a Dickens novel. He was a dreadful moaner and had a peculiar way of talking so my mother used to love going in there just to hear him speak. He sold nails and screws and the like, and the price always seemed to be the same. 'Three 'a' pence', (three half-pennies) he'd say.

On the corner of St Lawrence Road and opposite Morton & Reeves there was a sort of antiques/second-hand shop. As a child it always seemed eerie to me as the husband and wife who ran it were very tall and the man wore a long black coat and hat. He must have been very kind, because I once bought my mother a birthday present from there. It was a pair of Victorian vases marked up for £16 but he let me have them for £12 6s, which was all the money I had. He put them in a turkey bag – that's a sort of long, plaited-straw bag that butchers used – so I wouldn't break them on the way home.

There was a United Dairies where Morton & Reeves used to be, and it is now a Spar shop. The UD had a depot at the back from where they delivered the milk. When we were living in Branfill Road in the 1940s we had a milkman named Bradley, and one day he lost control of his cart – I suspect he forgot to put the brake on. The horse set off down the road, the cart turned over and the bottles fell out, leaving milk running all over the road. He seemed to be very careless as sometimes he'd knock on the door and there'd be a crash where he'd dropped the milk bottles on the doorstep.

Station Road, 1928.

I remember Mr Abraham, the miller, because when he was baking in his little shop he was always covered in flour. There'd be flour in his hair and all over his clothes, so we used to say he looked just like a bag of his flour. He was very kind though, and kept cabbage leaves in a box so the children could feed the rabbits he kept in hutches behind the shop.

Maggie Ollington

Gaynes Park Road

I was born in Maple Avenue in 1946 and was the youngest of five children. My parents had previously lived in Wingletye Lane for some time, and are buried, along with a couple of my siblings, in St Andrew's churchyard in Hornchurch. The shops in Gaynes Park Road provided for the tree estate very well. At that time there was Oliver's the butchers, then Norrington's the grocers, the veg shop and then the newsagents. My mother would send me to the butcher for a leg of lamb, which in the 1950s cost 19s 6d.

I remember when Kinda's sold clothes for children other than school uniform, and when I was about ten I coveted a yellow outfit in the window. Then there was Vambro's on the corner of Springfield Gardens, which sold very elegant ladies' wear. There was a

Hall Lane, 1906.

wonderful deli called Edwards at the top of Corbets Tey – we used to go there for delicious sausages and bridge rolls.

The Silver Horn, which was in Corbets Tey Road, opposite Stewart Avenue, was the most fantastic ice-cream shop. The owner would open a counter onto the street, or you could sit up at the inside counter and eat these fabulous ice-cream sundaes. He made his own ice cream and refused to pass the recipe on, taking it with him to the grave. We used to go in for an ice cream after mass and I recall the owner as being a great tease. At that time nobody had a fridge so you'd go in there and buy what we called a brick of ice cream. He'd wrap it in newspaper and we'd run all the way home with it before it melted.

My sister enjoyed skating on the wooden floors in Woolworths so she got thrown out.

Pat Duffey

The Silver Horn and Chamberlains

I often had a chat with Mr Caldicott, who co-owned the Silver Horn. Sometimes I'd buy a 3d cornet from him on my way home from school – you could see the ice cream spinning in the tub as he made it. His vanilla ice cream was out of this world and although he had people working for him he always made the ice cream himself, protecting the recipe from prying eyes. You could buy his ice cream in blocks that were deep frozen. The blocks were in a cardboard box which had the words Silver Horn on it, and he'd cut the block up for you if you asked. Then you'd have to belt home with the box before it melted.

He told me he went to the Black Forest every year for his holidays. The business was called Caldicott & De Gorgis, but Mr De Gorgis was a sleeping partner so we didn't see him, and I think Mr Caldicott retired to Spain.

Chamberlains was a lovely sweetshop in Corbets Tey Road. It was at the end of the parade of shops, and next to where the BP garage now is. The shop was owned by Mr Chamberlain and I'd go in there to get a quarter of aniseed twists from my 6d a week pocket money. Almost all the confectionary was in jars which Mr Chamberlain had to shake to loosen the sweets before weighing them, using a little silver scoop. I also used to enjoy liquorice 'boot laces', 'telegraph wires' and liquorice torpedoes. When you stepped into the shop the smell was absolutely lovely and you could buy as little as an ounce of sweets if you were short of money.

Richard Moorey

four

War Years

Gerpins Lane

We had nine bombs drop on our farm land, mostly in 1941. I can recall the Battle of Britain and I was only five years old. I remember being out with my father and he had a tip-cart near some old elm trees – all the elms have died off now. The siren went and dad released the horse so it could run free, then tipped the cart up and told me to get underneath. I watched the bombs dropping over Hornchurch aerodrome – they looked just like leaves falling off a tree and I could hear the shrapnel as it hit the ground in Gerpins Lane.

I went to The Bell School from when I was five until I was eleven and then to Gaynes. The cloakroom at the Bell was bombed and I can remember Swan Libraries being hit. There was a bomb in Tawney Avenue – the details of that can be seen in Peter Watt's book, *Hitler V. Havering: 1939-1945*.

Bert Bonnett

Butterfly Bombs and Machine Guns

We children were always being warned about butterfly bombs – they were so-named because they had wings on the sides. The bombs didn't explode when they hit the ground, but if anyone tried to pick them up or touch the wings, they went off causing terrible injuries.

Upminster was quite hectic during war time. Being so near to Hornchurch it was in the line of fire so to speak. I can remember being machine-gunned one day as I was walking along Corbets Tey Road. I looked up as I heard the noise and could see the sparks coming from the guns of an aircraft. My mother and I ran into Ports, the florists. All the pedestrians ran into the shops until the plane had passed. Bombers sometimes offloaded their bombs on us so they could return home empty.

We didn't have a decent night's sleep for years as we'd hear the siren go, then run to the Anderson shelter. The sky would be alight with searchlights, and guns would be banging away as we went out into the garden. I can still remember the awful dank smell of the shelter and the paraffin heater we used down there.

Planes used to hold dog fights over the Avon Road area which at that time was mainly fields. There were concrete public shelters in Station Road, one on either side of the road.

Maggie Ollington

Cranham Cottage

During the Second World War a bomb dropped in the field behind Cranham Cottage, where we lived, and our home was completely destroyed. Fortunately, my parents were visiting relatives at the time and I'd been evacuated to Yorkshire with my baby son. Luckily, the owner of the cottage also had a house in Clay Tye Road which my parents were able to move into.

My dad worked for Roomes for many years as despatch manager and used to be in the Home Guard with David Roome. When I fire-watched during the war, our base was in Gidden's wood yard. That was where I learned to play cards, as most of the planes used to fly across Upminster in the hope of dropping bombs on Hornchurch aerodrome, so I didn't get called out to any fires.

Bess Anglin

The Vet's War

Soon after the war began I joined the Home Guard and we were stationed in the old school in Station Road – I think it was called the British School. It took up a lot of my time and we had very good training. We'd march to Weald Park where there were weekend camps, and we learned to use live ammunition. We were also taught to shoot on Rainham Marshes and I was made lance-corporal of the Corbets Tey section – it consisted mainly of all the farm boys, so they knew me. For the first year of the war not a lot happened. It was very quiet and during that time we had a concrete shelter built in the garden. It was only 5ft x 6ft but it got to the stage when we had to sleep in it. One day we emerged from the

Harwood Hall Lane, *c.* 1900s.

shelter to be told by Mr Mercer that there were two unexploded bombs in the vacant plot about five houses along from us, so we should get out of the immediate vicinity quickly. Old Padstow, the farmer from Upminster, came along just then and said we could go with him, as by that time we had a small baby. No sooner had he spoken than there was an almighty explosion and the bombs went off, with the two houses either side of the plot crumbling like packs of cards.

Planes used to fly straight over the roof of our house from the Hornchurch aerodrome; in a bad way; it was an exciting time really. We used to fire-watch one night a week and I did very well for food, as farmers would put vegetables in my car and the odd joint of meat. We were given eggs galore. When the war really got going it affected our practice disastrously – Jean went to stay in Scotland with the baby and the local children were evacuated. People panicked and started having their dogs put down and I had a terrible time disposing of the bodies. People thought we were going to be blasted to bits and it was the Ministry of Agriculture contracts that kept me going really, with the regular inspection of dairy herds and the like.

I used to look after the horse belonging to Mr Fisk of Harwood Hall and one day it wandered into the lake. We had a job to get it out as it was stuck in the mud and we tried to help it with the guns blazing away – that was a terrible night. We called the fire brigade and although the horse didn't appear to be hurt, it always had a weak neck after that. The Army had guns located in South Ockendon and Berwick Pond Road and they'd blast away all night. We saw a lot of action during the Battle of Britain.

On one Saturday morning we were going to visit my parents in Grays and we got as far as South Ockendon when the guns started firing. As we drove through the country lanes there seemed to be planes above us with every turn we took. Our boys were either side of a German squadron and when we got as far as Field House Farm we ran in to Mr Algie, and sheltered in his cellar for quite a long time. When we got out it was very dark – the sky was black with smoke and there were little bits of paper falling down. That was the day the London Docks were severely bombed. It was just awful.

It was very cold in the concrete shelter in the garden so we bought a Morrison so we could stay in the house. One night we were sleeping downstairs when the warning went and we heard this most terrible noise, like nothing we'd heard before. We leaned over Ian's cot to shelter him from whatever was coming and it proved to be a German plane that had been struck over Stanford le Hope. It landed on a shelter in Hornchurch near Ravenscroft Drive, and everybody was killed.

A flying bomb brought down houses in Springfield Gardens. It shifted the roof of our house but we didn't know until we came to sell it and a got the results of the survey. A bomb came down between the two blocks of shops in Corbets Tey Road and took a slice off one end. Even at a time like that we saw humour in the toilet on the top floor moving back and forth in the breeze.

Dick Wylie

Shelters Named After Animals

There were shelters in the playground at The Bell School and they were identified by different animals. When the siren went, you knew which shelter to run to after grabbing your gasmask. I was a kangaroo. The teachers had a terrible time keeping the boys inside because when they heard the sound of a Doodlebug, they wanted to go out into the playground to watch it flying. There was a very large shelter at one end of the playground and for some reason it filled up with water. The staff had already put wooden seats in there, so the boys had a wonderful time. They sat on the benches, paddling away, pretending they were in canoes.

When the war was on, we lived in Southview Drive and the Home Guard took over our garage to use as a base. We had a Morrison shelter in the dining room and mother used to sleep in it when our baby brother was born – if the siren went off we'd jump in there with her. After a raid we'd get up the next morning to collect shrapnel and I still have some of it.

A firebomb hit the block of flats over the shops near Swan library. When you're at the opposite side of the road, you can see the lines of different coloured brickwork where the whole of the corner was demolished.

There was the British restaurant nearby the Windmill Hall, which I think was run by the council. The menu was quite basic but you could a buy a meal there without needing a ration book.

Val Eland

Fire-Watching on the Farm

When the war began I was called up for infantry training, but when I registered myself as a market gardener I was made exempt and sent home to the farm again. I joined the Home Guard and was sent to Bedfords Park which was the regional training centre for the Fire Service. We had a little fire-watching section here on the farm, and at first we used to come on duty when the air-raid warning went and go back to bed at the all-clear. There was a lot of

St Laurence Church.

action in the area and we found we were disturbed several times in the night, so we put bunks into one of the little outhouses so the men could get some sleep when they weren't on call.

There were four men to a crew and we had an old car to pull a trailer-pump at first, and there were pumps on three or four other farms in the area. I helped to man ours, along with our lorry driver and a couple of men who lived in the lane.

We had an Anderson shelter out in the garden. A Doodlebug fell on Springfield Gardens and we were involved in that. I remember running up the stairs in the house and looking at a hole in the wall. With all the destruction, the pendulum clock was still going on the wall. There wasn't a lot we could do but go to nearby houses to ask people if they'd remembered to turn the gas off.

I'm amazed when I think of how our lorry drivers coped as they drove through London when it was being heavily bombed. They risked their lives to deliver vegetables to London markets.

About seventy bombs in all fell on the farm during the war but that includes a stick of twenty. Fortunately we didn't experience much damage, except to my father's greenhouse – the glass kept getting broken as V2 rockets went through the sound barrier. I think we'd replaced about 1,000 panes of glass one day, when yet another rocket went over and our hard work was wasted. Father said that was the end of the nursery and he took the greenhouse down. Over the next couple of years he added a sunroom to the back of the house with the glass that survived. Despite a few cracked panes, it's still there, but we plan to replace it this year.

The best thing for me about the war was that I met my wife, Peggy, when she came to work on the farm. She'd been enlisted as a land girl and we liked each other immediately. For her, working on a farm was a big change from being a court dressmaker but she enjoyed being outside. Peggy and I used to go to the pictures in Hornchurch – the bus home terminated in Upminster so if there was a raid on, we'd run into somebody's porch to shelter until it was safe to walk home to Corbets Tey.

Eric Knight

five

Businesses and Services

The Policeman

I did my training in Oxfordshire when I joined the Essex Police Force in 1961. I moved into lodgings while my wife went back to live with her mother. I was initially stationed at Colchester for three months before being posted to Hornchurch. Although the Met had section houses, Essex Police didn't, and we were allocated a police house in Alder Avenue, Upminster, where we lived for the next five years. There were six police houses in the road and we lived at number six. After that we bought our own house and moved to High Elms in Cranham. I was still working in Hornchurch in 1965 when the Metropolitan Police took over from Essex Police and I was trained to ride the little lightweight motor cycles. They were manufactured by Velocettes but popularly known as 'Noddy' bikes, and it was at this time I was transferred to Upminster police station.

A condition of us opting to transfer to the Met was that they wouldn't move us to work in London. They could only do that on disciplinary grounds or if we applied for promotion. But we were able to volunteer to go up to town to do special jobs and I took advantage of that now and again. In those days we policed Upminster by walking the streets. It was quite a peaceful little place and we knew our area well so were instantly aware if anything was amiss. We knew all the local shopkeepers and characters.

The first transport the police had in Upminster was a minivan, and when they started bringing in the little panda cars – the Morris 1000 – we had to go on crash-conversion courses to see if we were fit to drive them. Later, we went on more courses at Hendon to be upgraded for different conditions. I remember we had a day's training to learn to tow vehicles properly, as stolen vehicles and so on used to be towed to the police stations at that time. Before the Met took over from Essex we had two old Austin Cambridge cars

Eric Kite on the A127.

which were kept at Romford – they each covered half the division. When the Met took over, they brought out the big old Wolseleys which had a bell on them – some had the blue lamp as well.

One incident I remember very well was when an articulated lorry turned over on the A127, scattering its load all over the road and obviously blocking the traffic. The strawberry farm ran alongside the road where the accident happened and the people working in the fields helped to clear the road while we redirected traffic. The lorry had been loaded with New Zealand Cheddar cheese and the company which owned it reckoned that by the time the area was cleared, the load was considerably lighter than when it had left their depot!

I went on the Met's fire-arms course and became classified as a marksman which expanded my opportunities within the force. In 1969 there was an uprising in the British West Indies on the island of Anguilla. Shots had been fired so the British Army were sent in to quell the uprising, followed by a contingent of the Metropolitan Police. The island's original police force had been disbanded and the Met called for volunteers to police the area. I volunteered and was accepted, and stayed on the island for about three months. We lived in bungalows owned by the locals and didn't experience much trouble. The climate was lovely so we were able to wear shorts and open-necked shirts. As an authorised shot I took part in many serious incidents and also gave witness protection.

Eric Kite

The Policewoman

I wanted to be a teacher when I left school but my parents didn't think it a good idea. My sister was married to a policeman so I knew many of their friends. I'd also been to police functions with them, so gradually found the idea of becoming a woman police constable (WPC) attractive. I applied for training in 1967 when I was eighteen and was accepted just after my nineteenth birthday. My training was done at Peel House, which was near Victoria in south-west London. During my training I lived in Peto House which was a hostel for young WPCs. At the end of the thirteen weeks we had a coming-out parade and at that time I was assigned to a police station. I'd become friendly with another trainee, Carol, and we were sent to Romford. Since my home was in Sydenham, which is south of the river, I didn't know where Romford was.

When I first wore my uniform I felt very proud. Initially, in Romford, I went on the beat with a more experienced officer – at that time there were only four policewomen at the station. We did a two-year probation period during which we continued to train, but because we were so young, we were more or less looked after by the older members at the station. There was no housing for WPCs in Romford so we were sent to Upminster, where there was furnished accommodation at the side of the police station. In 1965, when Romford Division transferred to the Met from Essex Constabulary, Upminster Police Station became part of the Metropolitan Police Area 'K' Division, which covered the new London Borough of Havering.

I absolutely loved living in the Upminster hostel with the other WPCs as we had our independence. It had one double and two single bedrooms with a communal lounge, kitchen and bathroom. There was even a small back garden. We learned how to cook and wash for ourselves very quickly, although we were provided with a cleaner. We had a telephone extension, which came directly through the Upminster Police Station switchboard, and the PCs next door were inclined to get annoyed if we had too many long, personal phone calls. Since we were all on various duties we four girls were rarely in the hostel at the same time but nonetheless formed great friendships, as we were all in the same situation – it was the first time we'd lived away from home.

Inspector Honor Miles or Sergeant Edith Cross would often make impromptu visits, so if any of us caught sight of either of their cars driving into the car park at the back of the police station next door, there would be much activity to get the place in order for their inspection. As we were like ships passing in the night, a message book was necessary to

Lois Easter in uniform, 1968.

relay information about incidents at work that needed to be followed up. We also used the book to remind each other it was time to pay the television licence or it was someone's turn to clean out the fridge.

I remained at the hostel for about four years and it was closed some time later and converted into offices. I completed six years in all with the police force. I married a serving police officer and we didn't think it a good idea for me to carry on with the same job, so I left and became a store detective in the West End for a few years. I didn't enjoy that so much as the police force as I felt a lot more vulnerable without the protection of the police uniform. When my children were old enough I went to university where I got my degree in education and became a teacher, so I achieved my ambition in the end.

Lois Easter

The Secretary

When I left school in 1951 I went to work in the City. A friend got me a job with The General Steamship & Navigation Co. which was near Tower Bridge. It was a large company with offices at Tower Hill but I worked in a satellite office near the wharf, so had much more excitement. I loved watching the ships passing by Tower Bridge as they plied up and down the river. There were two pleasure steamers at that time – *The Daffodil*, which went across the channel, and *The Queen of the Channel*, which went to Margate.

In 1974 I followed in my mother's footsteps and went back to the Sacred Heart of Mary School to work as school secretary, and I left twenty years later! A man knocked on the window one day, asking if he could come in to look around, saying he was an ex-soldier who'd been stationed there during the war. I showed him around and when we reached the old hall he pointed to the floor and said, 'I slept just there.'

Val Eland

Squash Club

I did a few little jobs when my children were old enough. A chap I knew, Frank Hartley, owned a squash club just opposite the Bridge House and I did some part-time work for him. I also did some work for the estate agents by the station, which was called Tadman Baxter.

Pat Duffey

Lilliputs, 2008.

The Egg Lady

We moved to the Upminster Park Estate in 1958, just as the last of the houses were being built. I think most of the Avon Road shops were ready for occupation by then but some were still empty and the pub wasn't quite finished. I'd always worked in a West End bank but I left when I was refused a transfer to the City, which would have made travelling easier. I then worked for a City insurance company and stayed there for a few years, before we started our family. I've always been active and tried various ways to fit in a job that coincided with the children's needs. I trained as a beauty counsellor and went into people's houses giving parties. I made lots of friends in the locality, but gave it up to work for Lilliputs in Wingletye Lane. It was still a farm in the 1960s, and I took on the egg round.

When the owners gave up the farm in the late 1960s they were happy for me to take on the round myself. I covered Hornchurch, Emerson Park, Collier Row and some parts of Upminster, delivering eggs in my little Morris Minor. Lilliputs had a big shed where their chickens were housed so produced their own eggs, but I had to buy mine, and got them from Alf Turner who lived in High House at the end of Corbets Tey Road – he took eggs from a farm and sold them on. The eggs were in trays and I'd buy egg boxes to put them in, although

High House.

some ladies preferred me to put them in a bowl. The round took me three days and I'd buy a new supply of eggs each week. In fact an egg is considered fresh for three weeks.

At Christmas I'd sell chickens too. I think Mr Turner at High House sold chickens as well but I didn't buy from him as I would have had to clean and pluck them. I bought mine from the butcher at Upminster Bridge who sold them oven-ready. They were fresh farm chickens and in fact I think he got them from High House but was prepared to clean them whereas I wasn't.

Hilda Gant

The Librarian

Initially I wanted to be a teacher when I left school. I gained a place at university but I didn't get enough A-levels so went back to third-year-sixth to get another. By that time I began wondering if I really wanted to be a teacher, but thought perhaps not, and decided it might be nice to be a librarian.

I started work in Barking and Dagenham but found the travelling difficult so after about seven months transferred to Fairkytes in Billet Lane. It's now an arts centre but it housed the Hornchurch Library until about 1960 when it transferred to the new building in North Street. To begin library training you needed two A-levels or to have passed the First Professional Examination, which was known as the FPE but is a qualification that doesn't exist any more. You could study for the FPE either part-time or perhaps by a correspondence course, and there was a day-release scheme.

Just after that they brought in that you had to have either the FPE or two A-levels to get a place at library training college. I had my other A-level by then, plus I had the FPE, so when I was twenty-two I was able to go to library school for a year. There were two library colleges in London at that time – one was at the North West Poly but I went to Ealing Tech. I learned cataloguing and classifications, bibliography, administration plus literature as a special subject. I think perhaps I enjoyed administration and cataloguing best, but really I liked all the subjects. You had to be twenty-three to become a chartered librarian, which is a degree qualification now. Fortunately, just as I was coming up to be twenty-three a post became vacant in Elm Park Library and I began there as branch librarian, eventually transferring to Upminster Library, where I worked for four years.

Prior to becoming a qualified librarian I worked in the old Upminster Library in the early sixties and later went back there for a short while. At that time the library was housed in the Clock House and had been there since 1936. Conditions were very difficult as there was little space and light. We had to make do with using a very small room as a workroom, storeroom and staffroom combined, with just a tiny space allocated to the cloakroom in the corner. Mr Reading was branch librarian at that time and he was very discreet so used the nearby public toilets to save us embarrassment. In fact, we all used the public toilets from time to time as our own was apt to freeze up. At least the children had their own separate room but it was always dark and dreary due to its lack of natural light. Space was so tight that shelving books could be hazardous at times, both to members of staff and public. A tiny area at the front of the building was allocated to the reference library – pathetically inadequate by today's standards as it contained only a few periodicals and essential books with a couple of stools placed strategically nearby.

Most memorable are the creepy trips to what was known as the 'onion room'. This was where we kept important but little-used books. We had to go into the building next door by way of some creaking steps and into a cobwebby, musty old room. We hated going in there on winter evenings, especially since we were unable to have a light for fear of a gas leak. It's puzzling now that the potential gas leak was never investigated. Why the 'onion room'? Some gardeners used to keep their tools in there and I can only guess the space had been used to store onions as well. One of the men once put his foot through the floor boards, and a colleague recalls the building shaking when the clock struck in the tower. The old library closed in 1963 and I helped with the packing when it moved to the new site in Corbets Tey Road.

There was an ambulance station to the rear of the building and it's since been converted into old people's flats, so they have the gardens at the rear with the duck pond. Despite the awful conditions we worked under, I have very fond memories of that old building and when I meet up with old colleagues we have many a laugh at what we suffered – nobody would put up with it today.

Patricia Worton

Ford Motor Co.

My Dad worked at Ford's and, having been through the years of the Depression, he advised me that the only men who got regular work were those who'd served an apprenticeship. Because of this I became an apprenticed toolmaker with Ford's and was there for five years.

I stayed with Ford's for a few years after I 'came out of my time'. But I wanted to get off the shop floor and into an office where the money was better, so applied to Delaney Galley in Barking who made air-conditioning units and heaters for Ford cars. I got the job and stayed with them for a couple of years.

After that I took on a contract where I worked away from home for three months but when I returned I went back to Ford's because they were offering a salary of 30 per cent more. I had a wife and baby to support so the extra money was an attraction. I worked on estimating and processing in the body shop and also worked on pressed tool parts. I came out of toolmaking in 1966 and stayed with Ford's, working at their various sites for over forty years.

Alex Duffey

Roomes Stores

I was with Roomes for about twenty years, working in the department which sold glass, silver, cutlery and garden furniture. We were on the ground floor in the second, smaller building and I eventually became a buyer, which was really interesting as I took trips to London on buying expeditions. I loved working in shops as I liked the contact with people – I could never have worked in an office. I think we wore maroon-coloured overalls. We worked from Monday to Saturday, with the store closing for a half day on Thursday. Luckily at that time we were living close by in Howard Road so I could go home for lunch.

Bess Anglin

Eastex display at Roomes, 1991.

Eastex

I thought I'd get a regular little part-time job when my children started senior school, and saw an advert for a part-timer in the school-wear department of Roomes Stores in about 1972. I applied for the job and, having been interviewed by Miss Doyle, was offered a position in fashion wear for three days a week. I'd always been interested in fashion so jumped at the chance and loved every minute of the time I worked in the department. Later Miss Doyle told me she could see she'd put a round peg in a round hole. At that time, Roomes had a beautiful millinery department selling lots of hats for 'occasions'. There were glass cases around the perimeter of the fashion department and on the actual floor there were stands with glass tops where we had hats and flowers – we sold lots of corsages at that time. The expensive things were always kept behind glass.

Having been there for some time, the buyer asked if I'd like to go to London with her to visit the showrooms in the West End. The manufacturers would show us their latest lines, give us lunch and sometimes put on a little fashion show for us. Afterwards we'd select the clothes we knew our regular customers would like. On one occasion we bought a small selection made by a German manufacturer called Funk. There was no budget for ad hoc advertising so I dressed in the Funk range and the buyer took a photograph of me. In this way we were able to advertise in the local paper and the line did very well.

Then the position of manager for the Eastex department became available and I was encouraged to apply for it. I was interviewed for the job and got it – and loved it. Eastex was owned by Ellis & Goldstein, who were two Polish gentlemen who came to England and began making clothes. They'd done this in their own country and they also had Dereta, Dumarsel dresses, etc. As they got bigger they manufactured even more lines. Their Dereta clothes fitted ladies of a standard size while Eastex was made for the shorter lady. Their clothes are shorter from the waist to the hip and also from the shoulder to the waist. A shorter lady can always buy Eastex clothes, knowing they will fit properly, and the range is traditional and classic.

When I was with Eastex, to a degree, we had to have what clothes we were sent, but for many years they'd put on a fashion show and we had an input to the sort of clothes that were suitable for our store. I had to wear what I was selling so, as I'm tall, had to have my skirts lengthened from the waist – although the year I left they brought in skirts made in two lengths. Even though I was working for a franchise I was still treated by Roomes as one of the family – they gave a leaving 'do' for me when I retired, having worked there for twenty-seven years.

When I worked for Roomes, Mr David and Mr John Roome were the directors and they'd followed Mr Millice Roome, their father, who was known as Mill. David, who was the elder, has since died. He had an office just behind the fitting rooms and he could hear my assistant and me chattering. When we weren't busy we amused ourselves by making up poems and when he retired we made one up for David, which he asked if we'd read at his retirement party. John was still working a couple of years ago to the best of my knowledge. Michael and Stephen Roome are his two sons and Michael often writes articles for the Residents' Association newsletter. Roomes used to close on Monday so we didn't work on Sunday or Monday, but when it opened for six days we used to have Sunday and a 'floating day' off. Some of us still meet up for lunch – Roomes is the sort of place which instils loyalty and friendship.

Hilda Gant

six

Farmlands

Sullens Farm

I was wheeled into Sullens Farm in 1918 by my Aunt Nellie Aggiss. My mother was one of the Aggiss family. I was one year old and had previously lived in St Lawrence Road.

There were three Aggiss girls of my mother's generation: there was Annie, then there was Lily, then Nellie. As a sideline, Grandfather William Aggiss used to run a horse-drawn taxi service from his showroom in Station Lane. He had a contract with Sir Thomas Barrett-Lennard to take him between Upminster Station and the family seat at Belhus. There's a large roundabout now at the end of the Aveley Road, but in Grandfather's time there was a little cottage to the left. It must have been built on a dip in the ground as you could only see the roof. It was probably where the gatekeeper lived, because it was at the side of the gate which led to the main drive leading up to the house. When Grandfather got to the gate, Thomas, who was the gatekeeper, would have it open in readiness for the vehicle to pass through. Sir Thomas had his own conveyance but liked Grandfather to take him to and from the station.

Walter John Knight was my grandfather on my father's side, and his wife was a Taylor from Barnstaple in Devon. He had two brothers – one was Isaac and the other, George. Isaac farmed Corner Farm in Aveley, and George farmed at Cranham Place in North Ockendon. Grandfather Knight would take a sack of grain up to Abraham, the miller, then when it was ground he'd bring it home so we could bake our own bread. The horsemen loved their horses and when I was small, Mr Ketley, who worked for the Gay family on the farm over the road, would call out to me, 'Come along Master Herrick', and lift me up for a ride on his horse.

When Grandfather Knight died, my father was able to raise the money, which he later paid off, so he could keep this farm. He was very forward-looking and we were one of the

Walter John Knight married Annie Aggiss on 25 November 1909 at St Laurence Church.

Farmlands

Walter and Annie Knight with sons Jack and Eric, *c.* 1930.

first farms to get mechanised. We rented a lot of land at one time so had various types of soil and this meant we were able to grow a variety of vegetables well. At our peak, we had two teams of shire horses and a cob that we grazed in the meadow opposite. They were shod along the road in Corbets Tey by Percy Coe. Percy and I went to the same college. My father had a stall where Aggiss's showroom used to be, then opened a shop next door to Ports, the florist, in Corbets Tey Road. He had another near the station at Elm Park and one in Station Road, Hornchurch. Bush Farm was part of the Champion Russell Estate and we took it over in 1943 when Mr Bonnett gave it up.

When my wife Peggy and I married in 1943, we moved to Hall Park Road in Upminster, and later to Bush Farm in Bramble Lane. When my father died, Peggy and I moved into this farmhouse and my brother Jack and I continued to run the farm together. Jack and his wife, Doris, lived in Leasway. Jack is five years older than me because there was a little sister born in between us, but she died. At our peak we were farming in excess of 300 acres. My father had a stall in Borough Market, but when Jack and I took over we also sent vegetables to Covent Garden to be sold by the Gunnerys, who were our commissioned agents.

Nowadays farmers might only grow two vegetables but do it really well. They do it quickly in ideal conditions so they can deliver efficiently. Farming had to change. We began diversifying some years before my brother retired. He decided to retire to Norfolk when he became seventy, so I thought I'd retire at that age too, and did so five years later. In the end we were put out of business by the conglomerates, so out of necessity had to sell some land to the gravel people. We diversified and now run the farmyard as a small business park which is managed by my daughter.

Eric Knight

Sullens Farmhouse

The house wasn't damaged at all during the war years but there was some movement in the old scullery which had to be strengthened by another beam. My friend, Harry Wilson, was a builder and we managed to do that between us. The house is now Grade II Listed, with the earliest rooms being 500 years old. It probably began as a two-up and two-down,

Sullens Farmhouse.

and the original beams are still in place. They must have come from an old ship because you can still see the wooden pegs. The occupants would have climbed through the ceiling to reach the bedrooms, perhaps hoisting themselves up by a rope or a ladder, as there's no evidence of a staircase. The house was extended about 250 years ago and we've plenty of rooms now.

Eric Knight

Central Farm

My grandfather, Edward Bonnett, was born in 1873 and came here in 1920 when these farms were 50-acre county council smallholdings. His wife, Sarah Jane, was born in 1874. The smallholdings were primarily allocated to ex-soldiers, but although my grandfather hadn't been a soldier, his land had been taken away when Ford's wanted a housing estate built in Dagenham for their workers.

Lots of farmers in Dagenham and Barking lost their pieces of land in this way, so the council had to relocate them. In fact my grandfather didn't have a farm but ran a coal business and did other things. At some point he'd been a foreman on a farm in Ilford, so brought his family over to Upminster to work the land. The farm had been split from the Rainham Lodge Estate for about three years when he took over. The people who were here before him had been unable to grow anything because the land was infested with twitchgrass but my grandfather managed to give the soil heart. He grew vegetables because it was a cash crop. He had some cattle and because eight of our acres were a bit marshy, they grazed down there, as did his horses. He was a hard old boy and if anybody came here for lunch he expected them to work after they'd eaten.

People were self-sufficient in those days and grew their own feed for the cattle and horses. On this farm, osier rods were grown along the brook to tie up the radishes and so on. Grandfather had seven children. One son went into the coal business in Dagenham but later took over Bush Farm, which has since been dug out for sand. Another son went to Australia on the assisted-passage scheme and another, George, was killed when he was about ten by a horse on this farm. None of the three girls married into farming families and Lily and Millie moved to Kent. Ruby married a postman and ended up living in Derby Avenue in Upminster. Grandfather went to Stratford Market by horse and wagon. He'd leave at six at night and get back at eight in the morning – taking the produce to market and picking up manure on the way home. He'd get manure from places like the undertakers who would have used horses at that time. A vehicle was rarely allowed to run empty.

Old Jack Silvester used to return from market, then go out ploughing all day – they were tough in those days. But, they reckoned the horses used to come home on their own so the horsemen could sleep. On the way to the market, they'd pull up at the Ship and Shovel

Voices of Upminster

Edward and Sarah Jane Bonnett, c. 1880.

on the old A13 for a beer and sometimes, while they were in the pub, somebody would pull a joke on them by turning the horses round the other way so they went back home. I suppose they were all youngish chaps and had to have a joke. It was a hard life and sometimes they'd be so cold they'd walk beside the horse to keep warm instead of riding on the cart.

This farm has always been called Central Farm and Dad obviously worked for Grandfather for some of the time, but he also worked for my uncle up in Dagenham doing the coal job.

Dad, Albert Bonnett, was born in 1904 and he took the farm over from my grandfather in 1933. At that time my grandparents bought 5 acres of land from the council and built

At work in the fields, 1980.

the house which is in Gerpins Lane on the right-hand side just past the dust shoot. The house was built by Mulley's who were builders at the time but only do the undertaking now. Grandfather died in 1951 and Grandmother died exactly seven years later on the same date – 7 May. My dad was the only one who really came back here to work. He couldn't read or write much – I can recall him doing his sums on an old Tate & Lyle sugar bag and he used to draw things to make himself understood. I was born on 12 June 1935 and am the eldest of my family. One of my brothers was with us in the farm business until he went out to Australia in 1969, because he met and married an Australian girl. He said, 'If I'm not back in six months can I buy myself out of the business?' and he didn't come back. We traded under the name of A. Bonnett & Sons, and still do. Another brother, Roger, is an agricultural engineer in North Ockendon – his company is called RGB Services. I have no sons, just two daughters and we've only got 9 acres now, so I think the farm will fall into other hands when we've gone. My father bought his first lorry when I was a year old – that was in 1936. Before that they used horses. The farmers had to get mechanised when the Second World War came because the men went into the forces.

In my dad's days everything was grown organically and we didn't use a spray until about two years before he died. We had fly on the cabbages in 1959 so decided to get the crop sprayed. We began to rent more land and had something like over 100 acres at one time. We had fourteen staff and a manager then, and did pretty well, but as we went into the eighties the supermarkets took our business. At our peak, we specialised in the summer in lettuces and spring onions. On weekdays I had to be on the telephone early in the morning to see what the markets wanted. You'd take the risk of not selling your produce if you sent what you like up there, so you'd try to work with the wholesalers. During the summer I'd have two of my staff at work by five in the morning when they'd begin cutting lettuces. I'd phone the markets to see how many they wanted, then I'd go out and tell the boys. There could be as many as 500 boxes of them – they'd cut the lettuces on a job and finish basis. Everything would go to market at about four in the afternoon ready to be sold the next day. They'd leave here at about six and get home at ten at night.

My mother was a very good cook, as she went into service when she was young. She worked for a well-known family called Smith who lived in Emerson Park. She began on 3s 6d per week as a girl doing anything and everything, and progressed to be cook – 'good, plain cooking', she used to say. Dad brought her a few vegetables in from the farm. She always got the worst of the crop – potatoes with a chip out of them or half green. She didn't get the best vegetables because he could sell them, but Mum knew how to get to the good parts. It was only when us boys began working on the farm that we used to slip Mum the best, but Dad had been brought up not to waste anything. We used to get the meat delivered from Parish & Summerfield's in Corbets Tey Road.

We farmed potatoes until 1976, when we had a bad year so stopped growing them. We grew sweet corn, stick beans, beetroot, calabrese, celery, parsnips, cabbages, radishes, and so on, but not carrots – the soil round here is no good for carrots, you need to be in Cambridge for that. We grew cabbages all year round. Bailey's over on the East Hall Farm estate used to pack our farm produce. We grew up to 7 acres of strawberries and people came to pick their own. It did very well for a few years but trade dropped off – probably because people don't eat so much jam these days. My mum died in her sleep and my dad lived until he was eighty. He died in 1985, which was when my wife and I moved into the farmhouse. Ernest Doe was a big name in farming then, and still is. There were a couple of families who lived in cottages that were near the entrance of Upminster Golf Club – one was named Barnes and the other, Goodchild. Both the fathers worked for Doe's because they farmed nearby during the war.

When I left school my father told me I could either have a weekly wage or be paid the same as the other farmers' sons. This meant they had pocket money with their mothers buying their clothes and providing free board and lodging and so on, but I decided I wanted a wage. I was paid £2 5s a week, and gave my mother £1 for my keep, buying

Bert with his cart horses, 2004.

everything else for myself. I was later to work harder for myself than I did my dad, as far as hours were concerned. In the summer we'd work from seven in the morning until five, come in for tea until five-thirty, then go outside again and work until seven-thirty. We rented the land for years but later bought some of it from the county council. Eventually we sold some on to Thames Chase and the trees they've planted recently are doing very well. The soil on any farm is as good as you make it and ours was rich as it was fertilised regularly by manure. I retired when I was sixty years old because I could no longer make a living from farming.

I bought my shires then, and although we earned a little money with them, they always cost us more. I hadn't been around heavy horses for over forty years, so I offered to help somebody out to get used to them again. He watched me groom and then put me on to harrowing, and when he saw I could handle horses properly he said he'd teach me to pass my 'single' and 'pairs' driving certificates. These certificates aren't absolutely necessary but since I'd be ferrying people around I felt it was something I needed to do and it helps with your insurance premiums. The horses cost about £100 a week to maintain which included shoeing them every seven weeks. A farrier visits the farms these days.

I'm happy so long as I'm working with horses. I love them, and when I bought a pair of shire horses and built a rides-wagon, I used to take them to all the local events, giving people rides. I've done the windmill, Pages Wood and Belhus Park. After a few years I had to get rid of the horses as I'm not as strong as I was and shires are really heavy to groom. But I like keeping my hand in with horses, so nowadays I do some work as a groom on funerals. Sometimes I have to travel a long way for a funeral and leave home at five in the morning. I get the haynets ready, then feed and help groom the horses, as they need to look perfect. We have to wear black with toppers so all this is loaded on to the lorry with the hearse and the horses, and then we set off – we go all over the country. Cribbs, who I work for sometimes, now have a white hearse, and with a white hearse you have grey horses.

The area we sold to Thames Chase has been named Bonnett's Wood in recognition that our family has farmed here for over 100 years. The wood is now open to the public for walks and I'm really pleased with the way the land has been utilised.

Bert Bonnett

Central Farmhouse

Our present house has been a farmhouse since it was built by the county council in about 1918. It's not brick-built although it looks it. It's stud work with expanding metal on the outside and then plastered. On the inside it had plasterboard which was made with laths and bigger plasterboards but it's all been changed since. When it was originally built it was put onto a concrete base and has no footings. The chimney was built up the middle before they put the walls on, but it's changed shape as it's been extended.

Bert Bonnett

North of the A127

We've lived in an old farm worker's cottage in Tomkyns Lane for about twenty years, with much of the house being original, although we've extended it since being here. Tomkyns Lane used to be part of Bird Lane but it was cut off and renamed when all the intersections were closed on the A127. The area around here is part of the old Great Tomkyns estate and the original Tudor house, which I understand has a minstrel gallery, is still privately owned. Apparently it was built for a yeoman in the fifteenth century before Henry VIII came to the throne, and was called Great Readings at one time. It had previously been owned by a member of the Branfill family, and years ago timber was cut down from the estate to build warships for the Navy.

The farm next door to us used to be called Little Tomkyns and they kept sheep there, but it's now known as Howard's Farm. Mr Howard took it over about eight years ago and uses it

Great Tomkyns.

for stabling horses. He has about twenty, all of which are used for riding. Horse riding is very popular in the area. There are several farms around us. There's Ashprington Farm which was previously used to breed pigs, but is owned by Mr Sutton now, and he also keeps horses. Then there's Common Farm where Mr Ward has horses, his daughter is quite a serious equestrian. There's also Suttons Farm, although to the best of my knowledge it was never farmed. There must be about sixty horses on Tylers Common Farm, which stretches from Nags Head Lane to the M25 – there's a bridle path that runs up to, then alongside the M25 and back to Nags Head Lane again. You can go round in a circle right back to Tylers Common.

There are also several smallholdings around here which are owned by various people, all on this side of the A127. None of the farms produce crops or meat any more; most of them have been given over to horses. I was born in London in 1935 and left home in 1951. I was sixteen years old and left to take part in a government training scheme where I learned to be a cowman/stockman. This involved working with a pedigree herd of Jersey cows at Great Leighs near Braintree. Taking part in the scheme exempted me from doing National Service and I stayed there for a couple of years. In 1953 I went to Navestock to work for Thomas Bere at Beacon Hill Farm and Bois Hall – he had two herds of British Friesians. While working for him I met my wife, Brenda, and we were married in Bentley Church in 1956 when I was twenty-one. I left Mr Bere after three years to work for Robert Padfield

Riders in Tomkyns Lane, 2008.

in North Weald Hall and was with him for six years. When I was about twenty-six, I left North Weald as we decided it was time to get away from living in tied houses and buy something of our own.

Eric Kite

South Ockendon Fields

My father, Frank, was born in the early 1900s and always worked outdoors. We lived in South Ockendon so were surrounded by fields before much of the land was redeveloped for housing.

During school holidays and at weekends Pop would take me to work with him. In season, we'd go out in the fields at five o'clock in the morning to pick peas, finishing at seven when I'd have breakfast and get ready for school. Peas have a wonderful taste if you eat them straight from the pod.

I'd work alongside him during the hay-making season as well. The machine would reap the hay and tie it into bundles and it was our job to follow it, gathering the bundles up to stack them upright in tepees so the hay could dry out.

I was born in 1950 and although I went to the infants' and junior school nearby, when I was eleven I went to Gaynes School in Upminster on the school bus.

Kevin Mallon

seven

Places of Interest

The Barn

The barn opened as a museum in May 1976 and my interest was aroused when I saw it advertised. I came to have a look round and found myself returning quite often and eventually volunteered to help. I found out a volunteer does just about anything – act as tea boy, talk to visitors, clean up, look after the little bookstall and entertain groups of school children. Eventually I was given a set of keys, so was able to open up. I've been involved with the building for about twenty-six years now, and the situation has never changed in that the barn is always in need of volunteers.

I am now in my fourth year as curator and, as such, I take care of anything and everything. Originally the barn was called an agricultural museum because, as this was a large agricultural and horticultural area, we had a large amount of farm machinery. Over the years we've added items from all over the British Isles and it now contains anything that relates to social history. The Hornchurch and District Historical Society was founded in 1958 and so, when it was decided to use the barn as a museum, members of the society turned out their attics and sheds to see what exhibits they could find. When it opened there were fewer than 400 exhibits – currently we have more than 14,000 – with everything donated. The building is owned by the council at present, but a trust is being formed which will not be part and parcel of the Historical Society, although all the exhibits belong to them.

The building has always been a landmark for the borough and is now a tourist attraction for London as per the London Development Agency, and will also be a major one for the 2012 Olympics.

Built in the year 1450, the old oak timbers in the barn have been carbon-dated to 1420. The wood came from Epping and Hainault forests and from woods around the local area.

The Barn.

There was an abundance of timber in those days, as trees were being cut at will to build boats or galleys that went abroad to collect spices and silks to bring back to England. But it's reckoned there was such an excess of wood that they began building large barns to use up the timber. This particular barn would have been used to store wheat and corn and to shelter animals, mainly in the winter. It belonged initially to the church and then to the hall – therefore to the lord of the manor – so was never part of a farm.

By the beginning of the Second World War, it was owned by the council and had fallen into a bad state of repair. It was rented out to an Essex agricultural firm by the name of Doe's but they were mechanised so there were no horses here. After the war, and because the barn was so dilapidated, there was talk of turning it into a restaurant but it was decided it was too much of a fire hazard as it's made of wood and thatch, so it's unable to be heated. Local people also objected to the noise this would bring, so it was suggested it might be an appropriate place for an art gallery. This idea was rejected too when somebody pointed out that pictures and dampness don't mix, and for obvious reasons the barn is damp. The eventual decision was to turn it into a local history museum. Restoration began in late 1972, and the barn should have been opened in 1974 but there was a fire in the thatch which delayed the opening until 1976, although there was no other great damage.

We've had bats living in the barn for at least fifteen or sixteen years when they appeared quite suddenly and decided to stay. They're here all year round and some time ago a bat society identified the types we have as pipistrelle, long-eared brown and long-eared pink. Since then we've found a dead lesser-horseshoe bat, so must assume we have some of these too. We can only suppose from the number of droppings we continue to sweep up that there are quite a few of them living here, although they're never seen. They live off insects and we find the discarded wings of moths and butterflies lying around. They live for an average of thirty years and the female has one offspring per year. The bats live at one end of the barn during the winter and into spring. They have their young down at one end and when the offspring can fly, they all move to the other end of the barn. After that they're free-flying and when winter comes they go back to the first end of the barn to hibernate again.

In 1939 a man hanged himself in the barn. It seems he was a farm worker who lived close by and he and his wife were always quarrelling. After such arguments, he'd go off for a few days to calm himself, so on this occasion nobody worried about his disappearance, thinking he'd return as usual. Children were able to crawl into the barn under the rotted door to play. There was little natural light but there were bales of hay, so an ideal place for them to amuse themselves. On that particular day two little boys and a girl were playing in the barn as usual when the girl screamed and ran out saying there was something scary in there. They went over to one of their fathers who had the keys for the barn. Armed with a torch he went to investigate, opened up the door and found the body of the farm worker swinging from one of the beams. I was told this story one Sunday by a lady visitor who claimed she was the little girl who initially saw the body.

A skull was also found in here at one time but there was nothing sinister attached to it and this is now in one of the police museums. It was found at the time of the restoration. We assume the barn was called a tithe barn simply because it's so large. The second point is that there was a tithe barn in this area, just at the back of St Laurence Church. That tithe barn belonged to the Manor of Gaynes (the lord of the manor collected tithes.) Another thing, of course, was the tunnel. Originally there was a sanctuary tunnel from St Laurence Church to the tithe barn at the time of the Dissolution of the Monasteries. For anyone on the run, there would have been a sanctuary knocker on the door, so for as long as you stayed in the church you were protected from the law. But, whoever was in the church claiming sanctuary, would wish to get out and they would use the tunnel to exit. Some opinion is that there was a tunnel from St Laurence Church to this big barn but it's beyond reason there would have been a tunnel a mile and a quarter long. Hence, the title of 'tithe barn' was given to the wrong barn.

But, there was a sanctuary tunnel from Upminster Hall to this barn which was in the grounds of the hall. As soon as Catholic members of the family or staff got word that Henry VIII's men were going to stay at the hall for a night or two, they'd use the tunnels between the cellars of the hall and this barn to escape. Any tunnels have now been blocked

Memorabilia in The Barn.

up for safety and we're not allowed to dig for confirmation, as part of the site belongs to English Heritage. The wolf tithe, or tax, was applied to anywhere in England where wolves were roaming wild during the Middle Ages. They'd steal animals and sometimes even children. So, the monarch at that time declared he wanted the heads of a certain number of wolves per year, according to the size of each manor. All one knows is this was the smallest manor in the area and the figure was apparently four heads per year, with Gaynes being the largest and so it might have been called upon to produce as many as ten heads per year. This particular tax only lasted for a couple of years as it proved impossible to implement.

As we know, tithe means one tenth and it began as a tax levied by the Church on the crops and/or animals that were kept on the lord of the manor's land by various farm workers. The tenants were provided with housing and in return gave back one tenth of their produce/animals, which was collected by the lord of the manor on behalf of the Church. The produce, or tithe, would have been kept in a barn until it was sold and the proceeds presented to the Church to be distributed as they felt fit.

Malcolm Cullen

Places of Interest

Upminster Hall.

Monks' Walk.

Hill Place

Going through some documents, I discovered an old notice of sale for Hill Place which is now home to the Convent of the Sacred Heart of Mary, and the description is quite fascinating. It's undated but describes it as 'a property especially calculated for the residence of a gentleman fond of field sports.' It portrays Upminster as a social and picturesque village, so I expect it was pretty typical of its time. Hill Place sits on top of what was known locally as Upminster Hill, although its formal address is 70 St Mary's Lane.

The setting is still lovely and it's easy to imagine the sisters walking along the lane to church in the late 1920s. In the 1800s the house, which is now Grade II Listed, had some impressive tenants. The original house, which used to be on part of the Gaynes estate, dates back to 1790, and was probably built by Sir James Esdaile. Sir James' grandson eventually sold the old Hill Place to William Nokes, who in turn sold it on in 1827 to Wasey Sterry, a Romford solicitor. When Mr Sterry died in 1842 the house seems to have been tenanted until Temple Soanes bought it in 1867.

Having lived there for a few years, he decided to rebuild the house and brought in an architect named William Bartleet from Shenfield. Mr Bartleet had been praised for his restoration work on St Laurence Church. So, in 1871 the outside of the house was extended and reconstructed in red brick with stone dressings to a muted Gothic style, and it's still much the same today. The entrance hall is magnificent with its black and white tiled flooring and huge concrete and marble fireplace. There's wonderful oak panelling and a carved-oak staircase but the pièce de résistance, for me, is the stained-glass window executed in the William Morris workshop to the design of Sir Edward Burne-Jones, the popular Victorian artist. There are three floors, with the top two having some fifteen bedrooms plus bathrooms. There's a master suite that has fitted mahogany wardrobes with an adjacent bathroom. Of course, large houses built in that era would have had bathrooms, when most of the nineteenth-century population managed without so much as an inside toilet. Downstairs there were two reception rooms, a dining room, billiards room and the usual kitchens, pantries, toilets and domestic offices. There were cellars for wine and coal. Outside, Mr Soanes had a coach house built with stabling for horses and housing for grooms. The gardens had flower beds, lawns and shrubberies, so the house must have been a lovely place to live in.

There used to be three giant cedar trees in the grounds until relatively recently. They were said to be amongst the oldest in the country, but sadly one of these was blown down in the 1987 storm and another had to be taken down when it became diseased, so only one remains. It's not clear why Mr Soanes left Hill Place but in any case it was normal for wealthy people to visit other properties they owned from time to time, so maybe he rented it to people he knew. Records show that from 1882 until 1886 Countess Tasker lived there. She was the daughter of Joseph Tasker, who lived at Middleton Hall in Shenfield. The countess was a devout Catholic who supported an orphanage for boys

William Morris window at the Convent.

in Brentwood, among her other charitable works. Ellen Willmott, the horticulturist of Warley Hill, also lived at Hill Place at some time and she set about improving the gardens, which I suspect had become neglected by the succession of tenants. The estate appears to have been unoccupied in 1890 but in 1896 the property was bought by Major Edwin Woodiwiss, who kept a small zoo in the 11-acre grounds. I'm not sure what the regulations for zoo keeping were in those days, if any, but he seems to have bred rare alpacas, erected three aviaries, and an eyrie for his two eagles, besides installing a bear pit where he's reckoned to have kept a pet bear. He entertained W.G. Grace, the cricketer, at Hill Place, but was only there for about three years – goodness knows what happened to the animals when he left.

In 1899 Sir Edward P. Wills of the tobacco family bought the property and, on his death, Dr John Storrs Brookfield moved in. He was a retired Harley Street specialist who bought the house in 1902 for £12,000. Dr Brookfield devoted his time to the care of ex-soldiers disabled during the First World War. Although a kind man, he was a strict disciplinarian who helped rehabilitate the men by getting them to work in the gardens which he loved. They were certainly spectacular by then, with a lake and orchards, a kitchen garden, sunken garden and glasshouses with semi-tropical fruit. But the property changed hands again in the spring of 1927, when Dr Brookfield sold Hill Place to the Convent of the Sacred Heart of Mary for use as a convent and school and, happily, both are still flourishing today.

Maggie Ollington

Upminster Hall

Upminster Hall is an original building with very few changes having been made. The flagstones in the entrance hall and bar came from the old hunting lodge, and the Tudor staircase and gallery are still in place. There are, of course, rumours of ghosts.

The hunting lodge was also an infirmary, and used by the Abbots of Waltham. The infirmary was reckoned to be staffed by about ten monks. The idea of the hunting lodge was that whenever the reverend gentlemen required a break, they and their huntsmen would ride over from Waltham Abbey and stay for a period of time to rest and hunt for animals. The huntsmen would chase the animals towards the lodge and the reverends would be on the balcony with their marksmen, who had bows and arrows at the ready, in order to kill the animals. The infirmary served local people as well as the monks and this has been established by the names on a grave nearby. A church layperson could also have been buried locally but the body of any notable member of the abbey who died there would have been put across a horse or in a two-wheeled cart (tumbrel) and taken back to the abbey for burial. The hunting lodge disappeared at the Dissolution of the Monasteries, and this was when Upminster Hall was built in 1539–1540 for the lord of the manor. There were never many lords of this particular manor, as although the estate was granted to Robert Latham in the 1540s, it was held by generations of the Branfill family from the late 1600s until 1935, when it was taken over by the golf club.

Any large religious building would have three fish ponds (representing the Holy Trinity) and there were, in fact, three fish ponds in this area. They were fed from a stream that ran through the centre of Upminster, along what we now call Hall Lane, to the religious building. The stream turned at the entrance to what is now the golf club and just inside was the first of the ponds, with the second being in the area just outside the barn (before it was built), and the third located by what is known by the locals as Monks' Walk with its line of trees. It's said that depending entirely on how you ranked within the religious community, you would get the best or most inferior fish which were kept in the separate ponds. Although this is a romantic story it could well make sense. The fish were prevented from swimming from one pond to another by netting.

There used to be an Essex barn adjacent to the barn still standing. It was so-called as it was unique to Essex in that it had doors at both ends, so carts could come in at one end, load or unload and go out of the other end. It was a granary barn standing on staddle-stones which were concrete mushrooms that kept the building off the ground so vermin

Places of Interest

Part of the Tudor staircase at Upminster Hall.

An engraving of Upminster Hall, 1789.

MANOR OF UPMINSTER HALL

NOTICE!

No persons are entitled to depasture Live Stock upon the Common or Waste Lands of the Manor, excepting those tenants holding land within the Manor to which rights of pasture are annexed. The Horses, Cattle, and other Stock belonging to strangers, and found trespassing or straying upon the aforesaid Common or Waste Lands will be impounded, and penalties levied on the owners.

Gipsies, Hawkers, and others encamping on the said Lands, and Damaging the Turf by lighting Fires or otherwise, will be Prosecuted.

BY ORDER,

W. C. CLIFTON,
STEWARD.

ROMFORD, JANUARY, 1885.

WILSON & WHITWORTH, STEAM PRINTERS, ROMFORD, STRATFORD, AND BRENTWOOD.

Notice of Sale of Common Land, 1885.

and so on couldn't gain access to the grain. Just outside one end of the present barn was a blacksmiths – there's still evidence of this by the pieces of coal that are to be found around the barn to this day. The smithy would have been built here for the lord of the manor as horses were the only means of transport, and although there was never a farm on this site, there were farms nearby. By 1960 both the blacksmiths and the Essex barn had been pulled down.

On 1 April 1918 the Royal Flying Corps became the Royal Air Force and the hall was the headquarters of 49th Group Fighter Command which was responsible for RAF Hornchurch at Suttons Farm, RAF North Weald and RAF Fairlop. The first commanding officer when it became the Royal Air Force was a captain, who still retained his RFC rank.

Malcolm Cullen

New Place

The Clock House

I became very passionate about the clock house at one time and still like to know what's happening to it. The mansion called New Place was sadly demolished in 1924, but the clock house, which had been the coach house and stables of the old mansion, was retained. The clock house was kept because, at that time, Upminster was run by the parish council who were a very democratic body. They were unable to do such things as borrow more than a certain amount of money without assembling the ratepayers and taking a vote. When they gathered to vote on whether they wanted the council to purchase New Place and the clock house, the vote was heavily against the purchase. However, the clock house vote was won by something like 155 against 153. So, the council was obliged to purchase the clock house and it was duly saved.

The parish council was superseded by Hornchurch Urban District Council in 1934, and they decided they had no use for the clock house. It had been under threat for years, firstly from Hornchurch, and when Havering took over in 1964 it had once again been in danger of being demolished, but I was determined it would be saved. When I was ward secretary I used to get what was known as the grey book. Copies of this were issued six or seven times a year and consisted of minutes of full council meetings and committees. As secretary I'd be sent copies and read them through to keep abreast of what was going on, just to see if anything needed to be reported to the committee. The clock house was a Listed Building and on one occasion I read the grey book and found it had been resolved that they would ask the leisure and recreation services committee, which had control of the clock house, to write to the Secretary of State for the setting aside of the listing of this building. I had papers in my possession that had come from the last secretary relating to the clock house, and it was obvious that only a year before, following petitions by the residents of Upminster, it had been requested that the building be listed by the minister.

I was perturbed about this and wrote to the Department of the Environment, pointing out the forthcoming application. I assured the department that the people of Upminster, having raised such an objection to the demolition the previous year, wouldn't suddenly change their minds and say you can get rid of it this year! This resulted in the minister calling for a public inquiry by an inspector the following January. In the meantime, the Greater London Council still existed in those days and it had an historic buildings division which was also very interested in preserving the clock house. The person from the historic buildings division heard about my interest and got in touch with me. He said he was delighted our association was opposing the application because very often they object to the demolition of such buildings and absolutely no one locally protests. The result is that the inspector thinks that nobody seems to care, so lets the application go through. The upshot was that an inquiry was held in the January and lots of us entered objections, so within a few weeks the inspector declared it should be preserved. For nine years the clock house stood with nobody doing anything with it until it was converted into eight flats for elderly people with the tower being refurbished and restored.

The inspector insisted on coming down to look at the clock house the day after the inquiry and those of us who were interested took a day off work to go round with him. We went out on to the roof, for example, which is mostly original, with 200-year-old tiles. They're probably handmade as they're slightly irregular in pattern whereas the newer ones are more uniform, having been made by machine. The top of the building had been terribly neglected with plants growing in the roof. There are two floors and the top floor was absolutely solid despite its years. On the tower itself there's a little cupola on top with a clock in it, and through the wooden slats we were able to see the mechanism with the name of the maker and the date. I think it's a very attractive building and now the doors and windows have largely been restored to their proper dimensions, it looks even better.

Geoffrey Lewis

The Clock

New Place estate is Grade II Listed and was built in the 1770s as the seat of the Esdaile family. The house was demolished in 1924 but the stables were saved and bought by the council to use as offices. The red-brick stable block is located at the front of the grounds in St Mary's Lane, and in Sir James' time the groom lived over the stables. The clock tower, which sits above the building, has a weather vane dated 1700 on its apex. Sir James Esdaile was a wealthy banker who also supplied cartridges to the Army so it's most likely due to his connections that he was able to bring the clock from the Woolwich Arsenal to Upminster. The clock was signed and dated by Edward Tutet in 1774.

Behind the clock house building is the 'duck pond', as it's usually called locally, with the moat and gardens that are part of the original estate. To the front is the red telephone box which is also Grade II Listed. The old clock tower was refurbished in the early 1990s and

Places of Interest

The clock house.

at that time the workings of the old clock were initially put into storage and replaced. The present clock is now operated by an electric motor the size of a shoe box. We have the original workings of the clock as an exhibit in the barn which is now called the Museum of Nostalgia. We didn't get the original clock faces, only the mechanism, and it was offered to us when the storage company (Public Clocks) wanted to give it back to Havering Council. It was delivered to us in bits and took two gentlemen most of the morning to reassemble the workings. All that's missing is the clock face itself and one or two other bits of mechanism.

Malcolm Cullen

The Windmill

Plans for Restoration
I used to play in the windmill when I was a child. I'd come over from Minster House with my friends and we'd push the door open and go in – this would have been in the fifties

The Listed telephone box.

and at that time the mill was left open. There were holes in the wooden cladding and rungs missing on the stairs but we were able to climb up the sides of the stairs. In our imagination the mill was a castle and we played at being knights. *Ivanhoe* had just come on to television and that gave us the idea. The defenders would be up high in the mill with the attackers galloping around outside. I have to stress we did no damage at all and if we played with any tools to enhance our game, we returned everything to its place and closed the door when we were finished. We'd be shouted at occasionally by people in the surrounding houses, as they were concerned for our safety – and quite rightly so.

Little did I know then, that I'd become a director of The Upminster Windmill Preservation Trust when I grew up. We became a limited company and registered charity in 2003, and are in the process of applying for a thirty-five-year lease from the council. When we have this, we can apply, for example, for a grant from the Heritage Lottery Fund. We need to take the lease since the council, as a public body, are prevented from applying for grants. In 2001, The Friends of Upminster Windmill was formed and they work with the trust and provide guides and more. Essex County Council bought the mill in 1937 and in 1948 a Windmill Committee was set up by some of the local people to take a lease from the council, but for a number of reasons the plans weren't realised. They seem to have disagreed amongst themselves and the whole thing collapsed.

When Essex County Council acquired the surrounding land and outbuildings for development in the 1960s, they wanted to demolish the mill. They went ahead and knocked down the outbuildings and steam plant at a cost of £3,650. A detailed survey was made of the mill at that time and the council planned to flatten everything and sell off the land for development. However, in 1961 the local people, and my father was one of them, made such a fuss about it that demolition of the mill was stopped. At this time The Bell Hotel, which stood on the town centre (it's still called The Bell Corner) and the bakery, which was in Station Road – opposite where Roomes furniture store now is – was demolished, and the heart of Upminster was lost. The council then agreed to spend £2,000 on repairs to the mill, which was to include rebuilding the lower gallery and replacing timbers to make the mill waterproof. The mill first opened to the public in 1968 and still needs roughly £475,000 to get it in working order again.

This might not seem a lot but it's in very good basic condition. The wooden teeth need replacing and the machinery needs refurbishment but most of the mill is complete and in good order. What we want is a restored mill, not a reproduction, and we've had millwrights down to give us estimates. In order for the Heritage Lottery Fund to give us the money we have to prove an educational benefit. The plan is to build a visitor centre on the site, a museum and a working interpretation of the mill itself. This would mean a visitor could buy a bag of grain and go away with a useable bag of flour. The foundations of the old bulldozed outbuildings are there already, so we have the base on which to build the visitor centre. Ideally we would like restore the mill to a position where it can produce flour for trading purposes but because it contains so much of the original fabric, it would no longer meet the required food regulations. To bring it up to present food health standards we'd have to renew a lot of it, which would mean replacing the original machinery.

However, we hope to get a set of stones working in the visitor centre. This is known as a Hurst frame, which is a set of electrically driven stones fed by stainless-steel hoppers, where visitors can watch their flour being ground. The latter would be easier to keep clean and meet food safety standards. I've worked in, and have friends who own windmills and lots of them would advise us on the restoration. The Society for the Protection of Ancient Buildings has a mills division and Mildred Cookson, who owns Maple Durham Watermill, which has been on the Thames since 1340, has been very helpful to us.

There was an infestation of death watch beetle at some time but it's now been treated with a preventative material and halted. Apart from a few pigeons in the loft and the odd mouse we don't get troubled by vermin. It's my opinion you can't preserve a mill without it being capable of working – that's the only way it will continue to live. At this time, we're still in danger of losing the site, as developers are already offering to pay for restoration of the mill if they're granted planning permission to build houses on the surrounding field. The mill is such an integral part of Upminster's history, it must be preserved.

Richard Moorey

History of the Windmill

James Nokes built Upminster Windmill in 1803. He farmed locally at Hunts Farm in Corbets Tey Road and his brother, William, was also a farmer who lived at Bridge House Farm. James had the tenancy of the field transferred to him before he built the mill, and it was a private venture so he used his own money. At that time London was expanding hugely because of the Industrial Revolution. The Napoleonic Wars were finished for the time being and Napoleon was out of the way in Elba. So, James decided trade would boom and he built the mill within just a year.

Then disaster struck when Napoleon escaped from Elba. The Americans bought Louisiana from the French so the French were then flush with American dollars when the Napoleonic Wars broke out again. It wasn't until 1815 that the wars finally ceased. It had been a very brave move to lay out all that money but James could see that the ever-growing population of London would need feeding and that Upminster was a superb place in which to build a mill. The main access road from the wheat fields of East Anglia came down through Colchester and Chelmsford and then Brentwood and on to Gallows Corner where it turned off into London. The mill is built on a hill so there's a good flow of air and he could perhaps turn seven cartloads of wheat into three cartloads of flour. He envisaged it would be much more convenient for farmers to stop off at Upminster with their wheat, rather than go into London where they'd have to queue to get their wheat milled.

So, James Nokes built the mill and also the cottages which housed the bakery. There was an eight-bushel oven behind the bakery, so the community could be baked for. He also was one of the people who put forward the money to build the old chapel, as he fell out with the old rector of Upminster. Nokes, who had lived in Tadlows and now lived at Hunts, led half the congregation away and they eventually built the old Congregational church. The mill was very successful and by 1812 it was working at full capacity and he had to install a steam engine, because when there was no wind the mill couldn't work. He got the engine from an old steam barge. The mill's rateable value had been £28 per annum but increased to £77, which was due to the increased capacity. The reason the mill still has the original wooden machinery is because they never drove it by auxiliary power – the old steam engine was at the back of the mill and drove a dedicated set of stones. Many mills turned over to cast-iron machinery which could take the strain of the steam engine; but not our mill at Upminster.

During the Second World War, the mills that had changed to cast-iron machinery were requisitioned and the iron stripped out, but the Upminster mill is completely intact. In 1812, when the steam engine came in, Nokes was buying in coal. Since there was no train service it had to be brought out of London by horse and cart or by boat to Tilbury, and thence conveyed to Upminster by horse and cart. As a result the local people came to the mill to ask to buy coal and he saw an opportunity, so started up the coal business. This would probably have been in the 1850s when more houses were being built. The coal was sold from big bunkers at the side of the mill. James Nokes died in 1838 and William Nokes in 1846, and the windmill and Bridge House Farm were inherited by Thomas Nokes, who was William's son. In 1844, Thomas Abraham had come to Upminster as foreman to Thomas Nokes, who was already running the mill. Thomas Abraham earned £1 a week at that time. However in 1849 the whole estate was put up for auction as it had been heavily mortgaged when Thomas Nokes began a lavish refurbishment plan and overstretched himself financially. It was bought by Ambrose Colson for £2,000 who sold it on shortly afterwards to James Wadeson.

Records show that in 1851 Thomas Abraham was back in Upminster and working in the mill for only 18s per week – he was expected to work night and day when the wind was good, although he would have run the steam engine when there was no wind. He left the mill again to farm at Orsett. But, six years later, in 1857, Thomas Abraham returned to Upminster and bought the mill and surrounding land for £1,100. He worked the mill until 1882 when he died, leaving it to his younger son, John Arkell Abraham. In 1912 John died and the mill passed to his two nephews, Alfred and Clement, with Alfred being the miller and Clement managing the business side, which included the coal business. He'd sit in a hut known locally as 'Clem's coal hut', and sell coal to the locals.

By 1916, due to government controls and the growth of large-scale milling, corn supplies decreased so the mill was unable to work to capacity. In the ensuing years the mill was badly affected by storms, and with no money for repairs it was inevitable that

Clem in his 'coal hole' at the windmill, c. 1900.

it would reach the end of its working life. I think the Abraham family held on to the mill for old time's sake, but in 1934 it was auctioned and bought by Mr W.H. Simmons for £3,400. But by 1937 it was for sale again and bought by Essex County Council. They planned to demolish and develop the site but were forced to change their decision following public outcry.

Sid and Bert Abraham continued to run the bakery until Sid died. Shortly afterwards Bert drowned himself, it's thought, in despair. He'd been offered just £4,000 in compensation for the enforced sale of the bakery and he worried that he'd not be able to support his family. He was heard to say that without him, there'd be one less mouth to feed. He was last seen riding his bicycle along Clay Tye Road towards Ockendon, and is said to have waved good morning to a well-wisher. His body was found later in the gravel pits. Sid had a son who died in a prisoner-of-war camp during the First World War. The last miller was Alfred Abraham (born 1856) who died in 1951 aged ninety-five. Alfred claimed he went up and down the mill stairs thirty times a day for sixty years – it couldn't have done him much harm.

Richard Moorey

Upminster Park Estate

Our house on the Upminster Park estate was built by James Rogerson in the 1950s. By the time he came to build those in our road he was losing money, so took one brick out of the length of each room. The result is the rooms are 9in smaller than the Cooper houses in Avon Road. My parents moved into the house in July 1955 and it cost £2,000 although my father opted to have a garage added for an extra £500. The Rogerson houses were modern without being modernist and had large wooden-framed windows. The rooms didn't have dado or picture rails and the ceilings were lower than in pre-war houses. On moving in, people began to individualise their houses and most put up coving. There was a double glass door between the sitting room and dining room but many owners made the two rooms into one in the 1960s. This was because they were unequal, in that the back rooms were significantly smaller than the front rooms, unlike the Cooper houses. This also meant that the kitchens were rather cramped. There was no central heating so there was often frost on the bedroom windows in winter. I've retained the tiled fireplace in the sitting room, and we had a coal store outside the back door which was sheltered by a concrete slab roof held up by an iron pole. We heated water by a small coal-fired stove in the corner of the kitchen and this was also useful for burning kitchen rubbish.

There were few electric appliances available at the time so my parents only asked for a limited number of sockets. At first we only had a wireless (a misnomer as it was

Upminster Railway Station, 1906.

plugged into the mains), a yellow Morphy Richards iron and a table lamp. By the end of 1956 or so, we also had a small cream-coloured Prestcold refrigerator and a Hoover washing machine with a mangle attached. It was just a tin box with an agitator inside it – you had to add the water from the taps. Our kitchen was fairly primitive by today's standards, with one wooden kitchen unit, a metal cupboard which held crockery, etc. and a red Formica-topped table. We kept nearly all our food cool in the larder and also used a meat safe before we had a fridge. This was still used to store the Christmas turkey for some years after the fridge appeared. The floor was covered with Marley tiles but there were cardinal red ceramic tiles in the area under the stove. Dark brown tiles were on the rest of the ground floor, which neighbours have said were also made by Marley. My parents laid carpet over them fairly soon but other people left them uncarpeted for several years.

They used magnolia paint for the walls which they argued went with nearly everything. Most of the furniture was still 'utility' even in 1955, including a pine wardrobe and two pine chests of drawers. In the sitting room we had a walnut cocktail cabinet with a matching desk, and a mahogany bookcase. Our brown moquette three-piece suite was from Peter Jones and in the dining room we had a mahogany sideboard which had followed my parents to Wales and back in the 1940s, plus a drop-leaf table. The most striking items of furniture were two 'cumbrae' chests of drawers made from attractive grained walnut veneer with modernistic cone-shaped handles and made in Glasgow.

Our first television set was bought in around 1959. At first my parents didn't have a telephone, and just after I was born in Oldchurch Hospital I was taken ill. A policeman cycled through the snow from Upminster police station at 2 in the morning to ask my father to call the hospital from the phone box in River Drive. Few people had money left over after paying the deposits on their houses, so had little in the way of furniture. One of our neighbours resorted to renting out their empty downstairs rooms to a dancing class. Although my father was relatively well paid as an accountant, my parents were still hard-pushed for money at that time. Dad was a bit envious of one of our neighbours who had a council mortgage at a fixed rate of 2.5 per cent, but everyone benefited from income tax relief on mortgage payments, a huge advantage when income tax was high in the 1960s. My parents didn't believe in HP (hire purchase) but like most other people we rented our television partly to ensure it was repaired quickly and to be able to replace it when it became outdated. We had about four different televisions between 1959 and 1970, when we got colour, and by contrast I had the same televisions between 1983 and 2007.

When they first moved in, the gardens were uncultivated but separated by wires and concrete posts. One of their first tasks was to get the neighbours to agree to erect a creosoted wooden fence along the bottom of the gardens. Sometimes neighbours took topsoil from gardens where the occupants had yet to arrive. Making the soil workable took some hard digging and most people began by planting potatoes to break it up. On dark evenings, my parents sometimes saw shadowy figures with wheelbarrows slink along the still unlit road with items 'lifted' from unfinished houses or builders' yards. We started off with a small lawn and a large vegetable patch, gradually adding a patio and enlarging the lawn, which reduced the size of the vegetable area. My parents bought four fruit trees from an old man who went from door-to-door selling trees. The pear tree was never very successful, the apple trees lasted for a couple of decades and the cherry tree reverted to type and became wild. The most successful tree was a peach tree grown from a stone.

Peter Morris

eight

Professions

The Vet

My father was born in Scotland and, because he was good with animals, his sister paid for him to go to veterinary college and he qualified in Edinburgh. He moved south to become assistant to Vincent in Horndon-on-the-Hill, whose surgery was in Grays. Mr Vincent's brother was well known for making motorbikes, and at one time my father had one. When Vincent retired in 1908, my father bought the practice from him. I was brought up in Grays and when I was about sixteen I decided I'd like to follow my father and had private tutorage to enable me to pass the entrance exam for vet college. I began training at the Royal Veterinary College in Camden Town in 1931 and qualified in 1935.

All our training was done on horses in those days and, as the railway yard backed on to the college, we were able to do our practical stuff on the horses out there. I was fortunate in that I was among the first batch of students to be taught to treat small animals, spaying etc.; in my father's time they only worked on large animals. Having said that, we seemed to spend most of our time dissecting horses, although I can recall dissecting a dog. In the final two years I was there they built the Beaumont, the small animal hospital in Camden and it's still there.

It was difficult to get a job at that time as there were more vets qualifying than there were vacancies, but I answered an advert for a vet in Cornwall and got a job down there. I only earned £3 per week but that included board and lodging, and it turned out to be a wonderful job where I got lots of experience. There were very few qualified vets in this area in the 1930s – there was father in Grays, Bennett in Romford, Barton in Brentwood, Biddis in West Ham, nobody around Dagenham, a vet in Rayleigh and one in Southend. There were dreadful restrictions on vets in those days – you weren't allowed to 'put up your plate' within so many miles of the next vet and there was no advertising allowed.

Students studying in the Royal Veterinary College library, c. 1890.

I'd been in Cornwall for about a year when my father got word a vet was wanted in Upminster and asked if I'd move home if he gave me the £250 to 'put up my plate'. This is the official term used by the Veterinary College to indicate a practice. So I agreed, and bought a brand new car for £100 from a garage in St Mary's Lane, and found myself a flat over a butcher's shop belonging to Mr Sibley, also in St Mary's Lane. I think it was number 175, opposite Sunnyside Gardens. My sister moved in with me to keep house, and I was in business. I was open for seven days a week and we had to bring the animals up the stairs to treat them. I've always lived on the practice so was on call for seven days a week during all my working life.

We had three rooms on the first floor and two on the second. On the first floor we turned the sitting room into a waiting room and the kitchen was my surgery-cum-examination room. Any dogs that needed to stay were tied up in the bathroom until we could get them to the kennels. Fortunately there were a couple of rooms upstairs that we used as bedrooms for ourselves. The owner at Folkes Farm had kept chickens but gave them up, so I took one of his empty hen houses and turned it into kennels. I had to take the dogs out to the kennels in the car. The Royal Veterinary College would only allow us one small advert, so I advertised myself as a vet and my sister put in another, advertising the kennels under her name. I got a letter from the registrar ticking me off about that but it was too late by then – the paper had already been printed.

The funny thing was my flat looked right down Sunnyside Gardens where a Mr Moss practiced and I could see all the dogs and cats going down there, while I had none. At that time there were a lot of unqualified vets around but people seemed to trust them so I found it hard to get clients. Mr Moss was unqualified but nearly everybody seemed to go to him, so I did my father's farm work. Father's practice came right out to Suttons Farm in Hornchurch, around Rainham, Upminster and Aveley. By now I'd met my wife, Jean, and in 1938 we were married and built our first house, which was 169 Corbets Tey Road. We bought the end plot next to where the shops are now, and almost opposite Hoppy Hall. It cost £400 which was an excessive amount at that time because plans had been passed for building shops there. It cost another £850 to have the house built. It had a room on one side which I used as a surgery and on the other side was a garage. At the time the shops where the hairdresser is hadn't been built, and the site was used as allotments.

When war threatened I received a circular from the Royal Veterinary College asking should we go to war, would we vets be prepared to serve in any of the forces? I said 'yes' and volunteered, but fortunately they had a surfeit of vets so I was made a part-time veterinary inspector by the Ministry of Agriculture instead. Lots of animals were killed and injured on the marshes during wartime and the RSPCA set me up with a first-aid kit and a humane killer. In those days horses were automatically put down when they broke a leg, as their legs are so difficult to heal, but nowadays vets do amazing things and are able to save them.

With the war over, we now had four children and although the main thing around here was the heavy horses, I'd built up a fair number of small animals. In December 1946 we moved into the newly built house which was number 238 Corbets Tey on the corner of Parklands Avenue. It was purpose built for a professional man, so I had a surgery and waiting room on one side. That winter it was very cold, with the lake at Parklands being frozen for weeks, and I used to exercise the dogs on it.

Since I was still helping father out and the small animal work had increased so much, I had to get an assistant and Dick Coulton arrived on 27th January 1947. Dick was wonderful at that time because he came to live in and used to help with the children, and for as long as I remember we never had a cross word. He'd been in the army during the war and ran a veterinary unit in Burma – he'd dealt with elephants and just about anything. Eventually I took him into partnership and started a new surgery in a house in Upminster Road, Hornchurch, and later moved it to Station Lane, Hornchurch. Dick died about ten years ago and the house has since been demolished with houses being built on the land.

In father's time he looked after lots of cattle that were kept on the marshes but, when Ford's bought the land, the herds diminished. In 1948 the RVC said anybody could set up a vet practice anywhere, so other vets opened up in the area with one being located in Stanford-le-Hope, so they took a lot of farm animals from us. After the war my father had a serious road accident so I had to get in a locum for his practice. Eddie Dixon had worked in

Dick and Jean Wylie, 1980s.

Olympic House.

the Hebrides so was used to dealing with large animals. Father died in 1958 and Eddie stayed on until some time in the eighties. But farm work was finishing because farming was a seven days a week job and they couldn't get cowmen as the men could earn more at Ford's. We had such trouble getting assistants to run the Grays practice we decided to close it.

Our own practice had grown enormously by then so we concentrated on Corbets Tey. In my day we used to spay an animal for £1 but it costs a bit more now! And we always gave a twenty-four hour service. Corbets Tey got so busy I had to convert the double garage into another surgery and waiting room, and even then we had queues outside into the road, which the neighbours didn't like, naturally. The house was originally built for a doctor so we were allowed to carry on a business from there. In 1979 I bought Olympic House which had originally been two farm cottages. We knocked down a lot of it and built the present surgery in Hall Lane, although it's nearly doubled in size since then.

Wylie Vets, 2008.

Then in 1980 I became semi-retired, having been in Corbets Tey for thirty-four years. My wife and I moved to Brentwood but I still went into the surgery in Corbets Tey for three half days per week. We weren't in Brentwood for long as we were always coming back this way to see our friends, so decided to move back again. My son, David, also trained as a vet and qualified in 1964, and went to work in Scotland for three years as he loved working with large animals. He came to join the practice in 1967 but he retired early due to poor health. We have no financial interest in the business at all now but the new partners asked if they could keep the name of Wylie.

Dick Wylie

The Doctor

I always wanted to be a doctor – I can give no reason except it was the only thing I ever wanted to do. I was born in London and went to a central school when I was eleven. From then on my education was steered towards my eventual entry into medical school, so I went on to St Clement Danes in Ducane Road, Hammersmith, to take my A-levels. It's difficult to remember exact dates but I did my national service from 1952-1954, before I began to study medicine. I did a couple of short periods of office work to earn some money at some time, and also worked in a laboratory in University College Hospital. Having done my national service I had to take the equivalent of matriculation with the main subject being biology. After that, I went on to a polytechnic to take courses in botany and zoology which enabled me to go to university.

I went to Bristol University, which is a very old medical school, and after five years I qualified, in 1961. I thoroughly enjoyed my time there and have a strong attachment to Bristol because it was during my training that I met my wife. She was a midwifery sister at the Bristol Maternity Hospital when I was a student doing my midwifery training. She taught me midwifery, calling me in at the last minute before delivery of the baby. For the first eighteen months in med school, students mainly attended lectures and demonstrations. We didn't see patients at all but studied anatomy and dissection. Then we took the second Medical Board examinations. After that we did our clinical work so started seeing patients in hospital.

I took my final examinations in 1961. I'd studied hard and expected to pass but nevertheless felt quite elated that I'd achieved my goal and was now a doctor. Not only did I pass, but won the obstetrics and gynaecology prize, for which I received £30 – but that was a nice little sum in those days. By this time, Norma and I were married. After qualifying I had to work in a hospital for a year, doing six months each on a surgical and medical ward. I worked in hospital for another year to learn more about obstetrics, paediatrics and ear, nose and throat. I really wanted to focus on paediatrics but it would have been a long struggle with yet more studying. As we had a child on the way by this time, I decided to go into general practice. Although it wasn't compulsory, I thought it a good idea to do a traineeship in general practice and, on completing this, my next step was to join a practice in Bristol – this was in 1964. It was a group practice where there were three of us but I soon realised that I wouldn't be happy unless I worked on my own. I wanted my own patients so I could take care of them as I thought appropriate.

While I was looking around for a single-handed practice, I noted they wanted GPs in New Zealand, so I applied, was interviewed and accepted. But, once my wife and I talked it over we realised we didn't want to go! We had elderly parents and New Zealand seemed a long way off. It was then I saw the advertisement for this practice in Upminster where the incumbent doctor was immigrating to Canada. The organisation that runs GPs today is the Primary Care Trust but in those days it was called the Family Practitioner Committee. The FPC appointed GPs, dentists and pharmacists, so I applied, was shortlisted, had an interview and was accepted.

We liked the look of Upminster, as from its position on the map it had easy access to London, although we rarely went there, and the coast. At that time I'd taken up sailing so it looked an ideal area in which to settle. So, we came to look at the practice which had a surgery attached to the house, although separate from it. The surgery had a waiting room, consulting room, office, treatment room and toilet. There were shops and schools within walking distance, so I accepted the position.

We moved in on 1st November 1966 – it was a very cold day. I'd wanted a couple of week's hand-over period but the previous doctor didn't agree to it. This meant I had to arrange for a doctor to take surgery during the move, so we had just twenty-four hours of cover, before I began work the following day. A few weeks later the local midwife arrived to say a mother having a home birth was having trouble in delivering her baby. It was a first birth and in my opinion all first births should take place in hospital, but that's by the by. I went to the house, could see the mother was in difficulty and that a normal delivery was out of the question. There was no time to get the patient to hospital so I had to act quickly. During training we'd been taught to deal with all sorts of emergencies but a doctor would never use forceps in the patient's home. But, there was no time to lose and forceps had to be used, but all ended well. The baby grew into a lovely young woman who sent me a piece of her twenty-first birthday cake.

Being so new to the area, I wondered what sort of a practice I'd come to as that sort of situation was so unusual, but everything proved to be all right. I had a wonderful practice and I feel any home or night visits I made throughout my years here were justified. One of the first things I did was advise mothers to throw away their thermometers. A child's temperature fluctuates all the time and mothers know when their babies are ill without worrying themselves about what might be a normal rise in temperature. I worked single-handed with a nurse/receptionist. My wife, being a midwife, did the ante-natal clinics with me and also helped with my immunisation clinics. In the old days patients sat around in a crowded waiting room picking up each other's germs and I didn't approve of this. I began with an appointments system, which my patients approved of, as they usually waited not more than ten minutes or so to see me. I took on the previous doctor's patients but they were at liberty to move if they wanted. I began with 3,300 patients and today an average GP has just 1,700.

Although the practice was busy I managed to get nights off by sharing night duty with three other single-practice doctors in the area. When we took family holidays I got locums from Harold Wood Hospital to cover for me. I was always interested in electronics and computers, and came up with the idea of printing off repeat prescriptions – mine was the first surgery around here to do that. I retired at the age of fifty-seven as I was fed up with the changes that were taking place in the National Health Service. Up until then GPs had a free rein to run their practices and take care of their patients as they saw fit, but when the government began bringing in targets and changing surgery hours and so on, I'd had enough. Nowadays it's all targets and you'll only get paid if you do so many vaccinations per year. I gave the new regime six months to see if I could adapt but I didn't like it, so retired.

I did a bit of locum work for about three years but the roads have become so crowded I spent too long travelling. In theory I'm still a North-East Area medical officer for the

Red Cross but I haven't had any contact with them for years. I used to lecture locally in the Red Cross hall in Branfill Road – I was Medical Officer for the local group. I was on various committees when I was practicing; The District Medical Committee was one of them. The idea of a single central hospital came up years ago and we doctors gave our opinion it wouldn't work. This, as far back as the seventies, and at that time our objections were accepted. But the government has other ideas, and now we have the Queen's Hospital.

I eased myself into retirement. I enjoy walking and carried on with the post-graduate unit work at Harold Wood Hospital before it closed. I was one of the founder members of the Post-Grad Unit – that's where doctors go to keep up to date with what's going on in medicine. It's been transferred to the Queen's Hospital now but I don't go there. Even now, seventeen years after giving up the practice, I don't regret my decision, but miss the people. However, my wife and I still live in the same house, so we're able to chat to former patients.

Dr Barrie Hanstead

The Undertaker

My grandfather, Bertie Frank Owen Mulley, started the undertaking business in 1929 and then it passed to my father, Raymond Herbert, and then down to me. I probably got teased a little about my family's profession when I was a schoolboy but it didn't worry me unduly. I always wanted to come to work for my father. I loved being around the activity in the workshop and the old black cars. I've always been keen on cars and to this day do most of the maintenance work on our fleet.

When I left school I trained as a motor mechanic until 1970 because my parents wanted me to have the advantage of an apprenticeship. But, as soon as an opportunity came up to work in the business, I took it. I started at the bottom and worked my way up – teaching myself how to make coffins on the way. Coffins used to be handmade on the premises but we buy them in now. We can't get the people who are able to make them any more, and it's a time-consuming job. If we want, for instance, a solid timber coffin we'll buy it from a firm that will make it especially for us. However, we buy in standard coffins en bloc and then fit them out individually to the customer's requirements.

From 1929 to 1969 the firm functioned as a funeral directors and builders, but about the time I joined we stopped doing the building work. At one point we employed eleven men and they carried out all the building and funeral work. There wasn't enough need to enable a business to keep going solely as funeral directors in those days. When grandfather started up there were only two companies doing funerals, just us and Wright's, whose premises were just up past the traffic lights at Bell Corner.

Until the 1930s all the small funeral directors around here used to hire a hearse from Aggiss's, who had a motorised hearse, and we all fitted our business in to when it would

Mulley's attending a funeral with horse-drawn carriage.

be available; after the war we all bought our own vehicles. I'm still able to maintain them. There's a lot of money invested in vehicles these days and we have a fleet of Mercedes. When we have requests for horse-drawn vehicles we have to hire them in. We usually do this from people who deal solely with horse-drawn carriages. Sometimes we get requests for white vehicles and sometimes coloured ones, or we get requests to match the colour of the plumes to the hearse. The carriages are made in Poland and cost £20,000 a time. We do pre-paid funerals now which on average cost about £2,300. This is something that's definitely on the increase. We're not allowed to hold the money – it's held by a trust company and it's possible to pay by instalments. Years ago, people would give money to my father in advance of the funeral, but it's not permitted now.

Fewer people have the deceased sent from home any more but prefer them to be taken straight from our chapel of rest to the cemetery. Another change is that people don't send so many flowers these days, with families requesting that donations be sent to charities. They ask for cheques to be made out to the charity of their choice and these are sent to the funeral director. In our case, we hold them for about a month then send the cheques with a list of donors to the next of kin. Flowers change in areas – more people send an oasis of flowers now, not the big wreaths, although in the East End you still get the lavish arrangements, such as 'the gates of heaven', 'cushions' and large crosses. Hospitals will only take a limited number of flowers these days as they don't have the staff to take care of them. If the family request it, we take ours to churches and to old folk's homes where the ladies enjoy rearranging the blooms. We deal with different religions now and will always adapt to suit the deceased's family's needs. We can cope with anything and everything.

Travellers' funerals seem to be larger than usual as they have bigger families and are more close-knit, needing numerous vehicles to accommodate them. They also like white hearses and white limousines. There are two firms in London that hire out cars for funerals and they both have a supply of white vehicles. We have a small company that, if required, will come in to embalm – not many funeral directors have their own embalmers because there's not enough work for them. Two of my three sons are involved with the business right now so we'll go into a fourth generation. Dad always said the easy bit is actually doing the funeral on the day, but it's the arranging and getting ready for it that's hard. There's so much to do, what with the paperwork and collecting the deceased from the hospital and bringing them to our chapel where the family come to view them. We still page the coffin by walking in front of the procession for a couple of hundred yards. This enables neighbours to pay their respects and gives time for private cars to join the cortège. Our responsibility doesn't end until we've taken the mourners back to the house.

We collect the deceased from wherever they've died. We don't just work locally but go to other areas, such as Southend and Chelmsford. If we're informed of a death occurring when somebody has been away visiting, or on holiday, we go wherever necessary to collect them. For instance, we've been as far as Wick in the north of Scotland, and Shropshire to bring a deceased relative back. We'll also do the same in reverse. If somebody dies down here and they had lived in say, Halifax, we'll take them up there. We also go to airports to collect the remains when people have died abroad and again, vice versa, when people from abroad have died here. The most funerals I've ever done in one day is seven. Years ago it used to be like that coming up to Christmas time when we'd often do three or four a day.

All the local funeral directors help each other out. Should we need extra bearers we'll borrow them, and the same applies in reverse. But all those involved know their jobs and the process works like clockwork. If another company's hearse breaks down we'll help them out, as they would if our hearse broke down. The only thing we don't do is pass on business as families like to stay with a funeral director for generations. Whatever the circumstances we'll always fit in a funeral somehow – even if we have to hire in everything and make a loss, we'll still oblige the customer. I sometimes get invited into the reception after a funeral but I rarely go as I feel people are more comfortable with only their family present when they've been bereaved.

I find my job fascinating even now – I absolutely love it. I live next door to the business so am on twenty-four-hour call.

Robert Mulley

nine

Entertainers

The Alto-Saxophone Player

My wife and I moved to Upminster in the 1950s, but I grew up in Forest Gate. I was born in 1921 and when I was about five my parents suggested I learn to play the violin. Although I was the only one in my immediate family to take up music, a couple of my cousins played musical instruments too. One eventually played professionally and the other was a semi-pro, so I suppose music must be in the genes. I managed to reach a good standard on the violin, but it was when I heard Steffan Grappelli playing his violin that I realised I wanted to play jazz.

Then I heard Benny Goodman playing and was so inspired by him that I persuaded my parents to buy me a clarinet. I always enjoyed music more than the academic subjects at school and although I played violin with the school orchestra I would never perform for my family. I'm not sure why this was but I understand most children are the same.

By the time I reached my teens I was doing gigs in local dance halls most evenings, and the money I earned enabled me to study clarinet at the Guildhall School of Music during the day for five years. Bert Weedon, who lived locally, was a friend of mine and we did the gigs together, with Bert playing the guitar. When rock and roll became popular, Bert wrote a tutoring book called *How to Play the Guitar*, which I think is still in publication today. We kept in touch for years but eventually went our separate ways.

My first professional job was with the Teddy Foster Orchestra. I was twenty-one at the time and he asked me to sit in with the band for one night, before offering me a permanent job. It wasn't Teddy's habit to audition, and the outcome was that I became the lead sax and clarinet player. It was while I was with Teddy that I fell for the female vocalist and eventually we married.

I was on the road for several years and eventually took a permanent job with the Frank Weir Orchestra in London, but I soon missed the excitement of one-night stands so took to

Ces Pressling.

Oscar Rabin and his orchestra.

the road again for a while. We didn't get much sleep when we were travelling around. We'd work until the early hours of the morning and had to be up early to get to the next venue, so usually finished our sleep on the coach. There were no burger bars in those days so we ate mainly in 'greasy spoons' and never missed a chance to stop off at Kate's Cabin on the A1.

In those days it wasn't like it is now with stars using limousines and sleeping in hotels. We travelled in old bone-shaker coaches and had to find our own digs when we arrived at the new location. I've been in some lousy digs and we certainly needed to love what we did to put up with it. Then, in 1949, Oscar Rabin asked me to join his band as the lead alto-sax player. During my time with him, we made hundreds of broadcasts and television appearances, and I stayed with Oscar for sixteen years, doing a solo every week. Oscar didn't front the band himself – this was done by Harry Davis who conducted the orchestra and made the announcements. He was very good looking, suave and elegant, and a great favourite with the ladies. However, having been with Oscar for thirty years, he left the band to join his daughter who lived in the States. His place was taken by David Ede just before we got the contract to play at the Lyceum, where we performed afternoon and evening for six days of the week. Although we were constantly working, at least we were able to go home to our families while at the same time doing what we loved. Sadly, David was killed in a boat accident some years later.

In 1955 we were living in Wanstead and my wife had just given birth to our second child when we met up with Roy Bull, the baritone-saxophone player with the band, who was living in Leytonstone. He said there were some new houses going up in Upminster and he'd love to go to see them. Since I was the only one in the band with a car he asked me to take him to see what they were like. We looked over the houses and Roy chose not to buy but I put down a £5 deposit on a house that had a garage – and here we are fifty-odd years later! After a while, Oscar's drummer came to live near to us in Upminster.

I played at the Lyceum in Tottenham Court Road for a good few years – Oscar had a five-year contract with them and in fact we were still playing there when he died in 1957. That was a very sad time for us because he was a lovely man and only in his fifties when he passed away. So, the band broke up and I joined the Ray McVay Orchestra, but couldn't settle and after a time decided to become a freelance session musician. Freelancing was exciting musically because I never knew what I'd be asked to do when the phone rang, but it was precarious financially.

During my time I worked with some of the greatest names in show business – Shirley Bassey, Syd Lawrence, Gene Pitney, Billy Eckstine, Pearl Bailey, Lulu, and Tom Jones, to name just some. I worked mainly in this country although we did some television work abroad. Lulu did her first broadcast with me on the *Monday-Monday* show. We were on the radio every Monday and Friday. Obviously we did the *Monday-Monday* show on Mondays, and on Friday we did *Go Man Go*. I played for *Come Dancing* right at the start and did it for years and years. Occasionally I still see myself on television when they talk about the old days and feature *Come Dancing* with the orchestras. We never knew what we were going to play before we got to a studio – we had to sight-read in those days. We just had to pick up our instruments and get on with it, but we were all professionally trained so it didn't matter. I've often contributed articles and critiques to musical publications.

About the time pop groups took over from the big bands, I was approached by Havering Council to take up the new position they'd created of peripatetic woodwind teacher. So I decided to concentrate on teaching and took the job, which meant visiting various schools to teach children how to play the saxophone, clarinet, flute and oboe. It was in 1967 that I was asked to teach the children music at the Engayne Saturday Music School, and ended up there as deputy headmaster. After some time doing that I was approached by Coopers' Coburn School in Upminster and remained there until my retirement in 1998. I started the wind band at Coopers and some of my pupils are now teaching music themselves.

Naturally I missed playing with the bands when I began to teach, but joined the Ken Turner Big Band that consists of ex-professional musicians. The Ken Turner band has been performing in Essex for years and years and I only gave up playing with them last year.

Cec Pressling

Entertainers

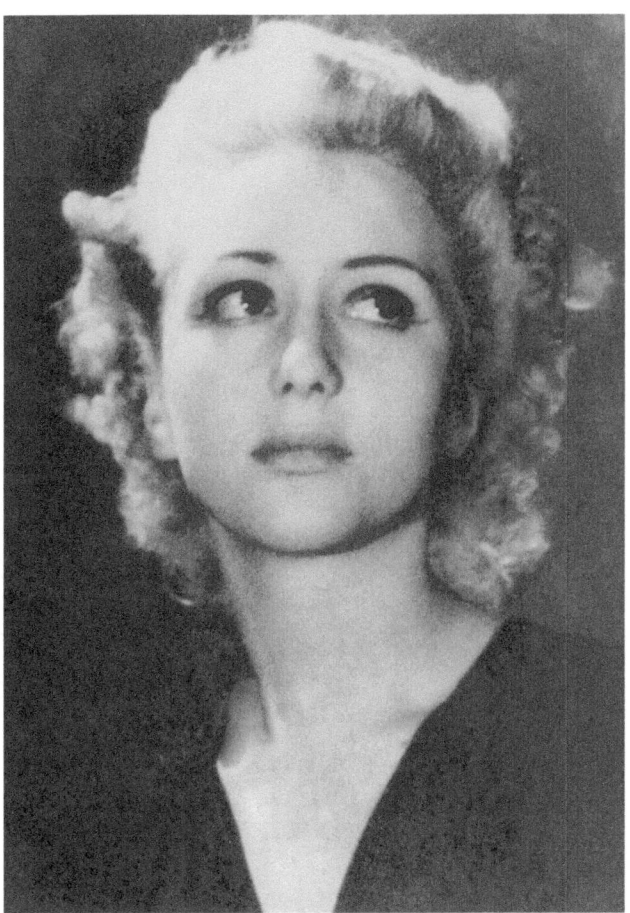

Jean Pressling as the glamorous Jean Ricki.

The Vocalist

I never wanted to do anything else with my life but sing and was in the school choir. I started singing professionally at a very early age – I must have been about sixteen – and began in my home town of Nottingham. I sang locally at first and then got a job singing in Devon. I saw a job advertised in *The Melody Maker*, which I bought every week, and decided to apply for it. As a result I became the resident vocalist at the Pavilion Ballroom in Exmouth and was there for three summer seasons. We went back there last year and it still looks the same. The pianist at Exmouth was Bill Paxton who later joined the Teddy Foster Orchestra. He was a very good musician who also played the trombone but, unfortunately, died later at the age of twenty-eight. Before that, when the band came to Nottingham, Bill Paxton phoned me to say they were looking for another vocalist, and when I went to see Teddy he asked if I was interested. Naturally, I was, so sent a tape to London and received

The Teddy Foster Orchestra.

a telegram by return, inviting me to join the Teddy Foster Orchestra and my very first engagement was broadcast.

My parents were very happy for me although my father sent me off with the words of caution: 'I'll only give you one bit of advice before you go and that's never do anything you'd be ashamed to tell your parents about', and I never forgot his advice, nor let him down.

Teddy was a Londoner who began his musical career by teaching the piano and then took to the drums, but he had a lovely husky singing voice and it was for this that he became well known. He worked hard to create a team of professionals and eventually led them to become one of the great bands of the time. Cec was working with the Teddy Foster Orchestra at the time so that's how we met.

I sang under the professional name of Jean Ricki and the men in the bands were wonderful to me, with only one person ever making an unwelcome pass. That said, they didn't look after me – I looked after them. I used to mother them, sewing on their buttons, ironing their shirts and so on, and nursed them when they were ill. I can even remember writing love letters to their girlfriends. Syd Lawrence, Jimmy Staples and, of course, Cec, were among some of the boys.

The first time I ever toured with the band I realised we were responsible for finding our own accommodation. We were tired and hungry when we arrived at the venue in Scotland which was a bit off the beaten track. We were becoming desperate to find somewhere to stay for the night and due to open in half an hour, when we finally we found one large room between us. The three men slept in the bed and I slept on the couch with a curtain draped around it.

While I was with Teddy we toured abroad and performed in such countries as Austria, Italy and Germany. The men in the band were a great bunch and I loved those days. I was offered a recording contract whilst we were in Italy but the thought of staying out there on my own, without the backing of the boys in the band, was a bit daunting, so I turned it down. Diana Coupland, who went on to find fame in *Bless This House*, was the other vocalist – most bands had one male singer and two girls.

Then Cec and I got engaged, and after some time I was offered a job back home in Nottingham. The Ken Macintosh Band was playing at the Astoria Ballroom and I joined them as their vocalist but then I got married and had children, so that was the end of my career. I think I regretted giving up singing later on, but I realise there was nothing else I could have done. I had children and Cec was on tour up and down the country, so sometimes I didn't see him for a month at a time, and babies need stability. I couldn't take them to places that were strange to them.

Later, when Cec was teaching, it was amazing how many children came to him with breathing problems, particularly asthma. Once they learned to play a woodwind instrument their condition improved no end as it's such good exercise for the lungs. He started a little orchestra at Engayne School, and for his first school concert had five children playing the clarinet to the tune of 'Strangers in the Night'. The audience was so moved they called for three encores. He was a wonderful teacher.

Because I was on my own for such long periods when Cec was away touring, I began to buy magazines and go in for competitions. Sometimes a caption would be called for and I began to win. In fact, I won a lot of very nice prizes such as three cars, eighteen holidays, television sets, freezers, furniture, bicycles and goodness knows what, right down to teacloths. Since I was winning so much, I decided it was time to have proper writing lessons and took a course locally. The first article I ever wrote was accepted by *Woman's Own* and I never looked back really. I continued to write short stories, articles and fillers for magazines, and then concentrated on television scripts. I wrote comedy for German television for years. I also wrote for British television and radio, working on productions such as the *Russ Abbot Show*, *Hale & Pace*, *Naked Video*, and others. As the market changed I became a teacher of writing myself, and still teach for just one day a week.

But Cec is the star of the show. He was a wonderful musician and acknowledged as one of the country's leading alto-sax players. In fact, on Portsmouth Radio last year, somebody did a tribute to the big bands and at one time they featured the Oscar Rabin Band. They spoke of Cec as an Oscar Rabin legend, one of the country's finest saxophonists, which made his family so very proud and moved us to tears. Even though I had to give up my singing ambitions, I've always been involved with the big bands through Cec, and most of our friends are musicians, so life has been very interesting.

Jean Pressling

The Film Extra

I'm still on the committee of the Essex Shire Horse Association and one day one of my friends asked me to help him take four horses up to Rickmansworth – adding that we had to try out a big vehicle for a blockbuster movie, so I agreed. The job was for Ridley Scott, the director, and when we arrived, he gave us some instructions which we completed to his satisfaction. The man who supplies most of the horses in the country was there and he told us to go Shepperton to get measured up. This happened, and we were dressed in Roman clothes. I always remember we wore boots with no heels and had to stand in a tub of dirt and water so we could get them muddy. Anyway, the outcome was I was in the film *Gladiator*, although I didn't have a clue at the time. Most of the film was made in Malta and Morocco. I did a few different films after that and used one of my own horses in *My Uncle Silas* with Albert Finney, one of the most genuine men I've ever met.

Bert Bonnett

ten

Reflections

Fogs

I remember the dreadful fogs when I was a child – sometimes we had to turn back home – they were so bad. At one time we children were lost in thick fog in Upminster Park but eventually found the tennis court, so we were able to get our bearings and make our way home.

Pat Duffey

Sunday School

The little building by the mini-roundabout at the Aveley Road end of Harwood Hall Lane was a Congregational chapel in my dad's day, and he was the Sunday school superintendent. It was an offshoot of the Congregational church in the town centre, and at one time there were sixty children on the books for Sunday school. This was where we learned about morals and behaving ourselves. Children would come streaming down from Corbets Tey village and surrounding areas, as Sunday school in those days was traditional. The chapel held a service in the evening which was well attended too. The old building is used as a day nursery now and just alongside there were two cottages, although they've since been made into one house. When we were first married, my wife, Pam, and I lived in one half. There were no sanitary arrangements at all, and that was as recent as fifty years ago.

I was twelve when my father bought me a bike from Sissleys, the cycle shop, and one day I was coming down Corbets Tey Road near Woolworths, giving my friend a ride on the crossbar, when I had the misfortune to come across a policeman. He gave me a thorough ticking off, but nowadays children ride on the pavements all the time.

Sissleys advertisement.

The George Inn, Corbets Tey.

There was a blacksmith's shop in Corbets Tey – if you're coming up the hill towards Corbets Tey there's the big cottage on the bend, then there's a cottage that lays back and the blacksmith's was just at the side of it. I used to take the horses to be shod up there for my dad. They charged 12s 6d for a set of shoes, but now it costs £100. It always costs more for a big shire horse because it can weigh about a ton, so has big hoofs. Percy Coe, the blacksmith, closed in the mid-1950s.

When I left school I came straight to work on the farm. I'd been working here for years already – every summer holiday, every evening – Dad didn't like anybody hanging about, and it was natural for us to go to work. My friends at school used to wait for half-term in the October because that was when we were potato harvesting and they'd come down to earn a few shillings. Nobody worried about working in those days because it was an accepted thing.

National Service did a lot for me. I had two years in the Air Force as a chef where the training was terrific. I mixed with people from all walks of life and when we were put together in a billet we had to get on. I played some of the best cricket of my life when I was in the RAF. I got into the maintenance command side where there were some very good amateur and professional cricketers.

One day, I walked into RAF Andover where I'd been chosen to work as chef to an Air Vice-Marshal, arriving six weeks early to get the kitchens going. As I entered the camp somebody yelled my name. To my great surprise it was Ian Gibbons, who I'd played cricket with in Upminster. With no ado, he said they needed a wicket keeper for their team and told me I was now 'it'.

Upminster has changed tremendously over these past years – I don't often meet anybody I know in the town now.

Bert Bonnett

Hockey

I played hockey from when I was fifteen until I was fifty-nine, and umpired for three years. I always played hockey; I think Upminster has five teams, even women's teams, and they play at Coopers Coburn School on Saturdays.

Eric Knight

Mr Gasper

Mr Gasper was the manager of the Gaumont Cinema in St Mary's Lane, which was originally called the Capitol. He was always to be found in the foyer by the ticket office where he welcomed everybody. He wore a dinner jacket with a black bow-tie plus a shirt with a stiff white collar, and he always dressed the same, even for the Saturday children's show. The cinema was to become a bingo hall, then Wallis's supermarket, then Gateway, and now Somerfield is on the site.

Richard Moorey

The Ducks' Park

Once a year the owners of the estate where the clock tower is gave the local children a tea party in the gardens by the duck pond. I can remember going to a twenty-first birthday party held above the old library at the ducks' park in the early 1960s. In those days they had a gardener on duty, and there was also a park keeper on the rec. They'd keep us youngsters in check, but nowadays children are allowed to do more or less as they like. Because of the vandalism, even the bowling park is kept locked nowadays unless there are people playing bowls in there.

Children had a lot of freedom in those days. Even at the age of four I was allowed to go to the park on my own, and I'd also go there with my brother to watch the cricket. Every Friday we'd go to the Capital Cinema and if we were lucky we'd buy a bag of chips on the way home.

Pat Duffey

The ducks' park.

Gigs

Live groups used to perform at weekends in the old windmill hall. The noise was deafening and this was my introduction to gigs.

Kevin Mallon

The Hunt

I can remember the excitement in the air when the hunt met. They'd ride off along Corbets Tey Road with the hounds barking and the call of the hunting horns.

Sometimes we went to Kent for our holidays to stay with an aunt. We'd go on the Tilbury ferry to Gravesend and then take the bus to Gillingham. We didn't see much of our uncle as he was away in the Navy.

My mother was born at 56 Elgin Crescent in London but she was orphaned when she was very young. She was sent to live with a very old lady who could neither read nor write, and whose house was on the green in South Ockendon.

My strongest memory of grandfather is of him sitting in the living room at Ivydene with his whiskey decanter on the table beside him and a glass. I can still remember the smell of cigars. In those days things were very formal and I'd be almost commanded to go to see him. I'd say 'hello grandfather', and just stand there shyly, not knowing what else to say.

It was probably in the early 1930s that Gidden's wood yard caught fire. It was terrifying to watch the flames leaping above the roofs from our standpoint in Garbutt Road.

Bess Gooden

Cafes

One of my duties as an elder sister was to accompany my young brother to the Saturday morning show at the Gaumont Cinema in St Mary's Lane. I hated these trips as the children made so much noise.

In the 1960s, there were two eating places in Upminster where a lady could go in on her own. One was Martell's, where the bowling people seemed to meet, and the other was the Cosy Corner Café. It was lovely to have tea and cakes in there, probably because it was at the crossroads and you could sit and watch people go by.

Val Eland

Avon Road

Married women could continue working in the mid-1950s but most women with children on the Upminster Park Estate were housewives. Because of this, shopping was done on a daily basis and children went home from school for their lunch break.

The patch of ground next to the clinic in Avon Road was reputedly intended to be the local library but the costs of the new Upminster library overran and there was never the money for it. The local Scouts had their annual fête on the land every year and would have liked to have built their hut on it but permission was never granted. Houses were recently built on the site.

Hardly anyone had a car in the late 1950s so everybody walked far more than they do now. The No.248 bus started at the top of Avon Road and went back and forth to Cranham via Upminster station. When the council estate was completed the route was extended down Avon Road and I think it then went on to Romford. The bus garage was in Hornchurch near Harrow Lodge sports centre, and you sometimes had to wait there when the drivers changed over. The buses were Routemasters, so had a conductor.

Advance Bookings for DINNERS DANCES BANQUETS WEDDING RECEPTIONS etc.	G. A. SMITH & SONS LTD. BOUGHT OF **THE BELL HOTEL** UPMINSTER ESSEX	TELEPHONE UPMINSTER 28 LUNCHEONS SERVED DAILY		
Mr. Noah 44 Southview Drive Upminster E.4.	27/8/60			
To: Catering for 78 persons @ 14/6		56	11	0
" @ 1/- (Teas)		3	18	0
Extension fee			5	0
Table Decorations		1	1	0
Band, Toastmaster as agreed		14	14	0
Refreshments supplied to house		5	0	0
3½ Bots Gordons Gin		6	15	0
7×12 Bots Best Dry Sherry		8	1	0
80 Players Cigarettes			16	4
2½ Bots Martini Sweet		4	10	0
3 Bots Orange Squash			15	0
2 Bots Cocktail Cherries			5	0
Luncheons to Band & T.M.		2	10	0
6 Bots Burlington Port		8	8	0
21 Bots Entre deux Mers		13	2	6
Off Sales Order as arranged		10	14	6
Refreshments at Bar		19	17	0
			14	11
Less Deposit Paid £5-0-0		LESS 5	0	0
Received Cheque with thanks 27/8/60		£153	18	3

A wedding reception receipt from The Bell Hotel, 1969.

I thought steam trains lasted longer than they appear to have done. I would have said we still had them in 1962 but history books say 1959. The compartments were mainly long bench seats – one on each side – with doors that opened manually, enabling passengers to leap on and off moving trains, which they soon got down to a fine art. There was no stop at West Ham, and Stepney East has since been renamed Limehouse. You could sometimes smell the fish from Billingsgate Market being loaded on to the trains. I also remember the bomb sites as we went through the East End with their vivid displays of fireweed (willow herb) and buddleia as late as the mid-1960s.

Peter Morris

The Councillor

I was very impressed with a comment my father-in-law made to me many years ago. He said that some sort of Independents should be elected to local councils so they could just get on with the job. I very much favour independence in local government. I don't see the point in party political alignment. There's no conservative way of cleaning the drains, or socialist way of sweeping the streets – there's a right way and a wrong way. I dislike party politics where councillors gang up and oppose each other for no good reason. They're there to get on with the job, which is to look after the area they represent. When my family first moved to Havering, or Hornchurch Urban District as it then was, we lived in South Hornchurch and one evening somebody knocked on the door and said he was from the local residents' association and would we like to join? When he explained what they did and that they were Independents who stood for election to council we were delighted to see him, so my wife Joan and I became members.

Later, when we moved to Upminster, a jolly character called Sid Pollard arrived on our doorstep and asked if we'd like to join what was then called the local ratepayers' association. Obviously it was the same sort of organisation, and it held the three seats in those days, as indeed it does again now. I was very pleased to see him also and, again, we joined. The main reason I became involved with the residents' association is that it puts up candidates for the council and indeed is the largest independent group on any London Borough – it has about thirteen members even now, and had more in the past. Not long after the formation of Havering – by joining Hornchurch and Romford – the Labour party had its one and only Labour majority administration in Havering and the first thing that happened was the rates went up! Not best pleased about that, I turned up at the AGM of the combined Cranham and Upminster Ratepayers Association and asked what they were going to do about the rising rates. Their response was that they depended on active members to try to change things, so what did I intend doing about it? Was I willing to get involved?

Reflections

Geoff and Joan Lewis in formal dress.

Realising they needed support with what they were trying to do I decided I would get involved. The next month was the AGM of the ward committee. This association is divided into two wards – Cranham and Upminster – with each having a committee of its own. There's an executive committee which is the overall governing body of the association. The AGM of the Upminster Ward Committee was held the following month and I joined its committee. Within about six weeks I was asked if I'd become secretary of the ward. This was rather quick but the former secretary had left some months before and an elderly gentleman from Emerson Park was trying to keep the job going and it wasn't very convenient for him. This happened during 1972. I held the ward secretary job for about two and a half years. The bulletin used to be edited by a lady called Cynthia and she and her husband were from a town in the north. When they decided to move north again to retire, I was asked to edit the bulletin and did so for a little over seven years. We lost the Upminster seats to the Conservatives in 1974 and the three councillors who'd previously held the seats simply dropped out of activity.

I was very keen to get the seats back so led the others in the fight to reclaim them. In 1981 I won my seat again, so served alongside two Conservatives. At the same time I gave up editorship of the bulletin. That went on for about five and a bit years, but in the 1986 borough elections we lost the seat again by a very narrow margin. In 1990 there was a big shift of popularity away from the Conservatives. National politics have an influence on these things and the conservatives were becoming enormously unpopular, so lost the three seats in the local elections. We didn't win by a great majority, but we won. In 1994 we were returned again – there were two seats in each of the Cranhams at that time, Cranham West and Cranham East. Joan was elected for Cranham West and I was elected for Cranham East. By 1998 the Cranham seats were won by a bigger majority and Upminster with a huge majority, so now we held all three seats safely. We had seven councillors in all to serve the three wards.

That was the year we retired from the council, and although I was president of the association for some years after that, once my term ended in February of this year I retired from active involvement. There wasn't much to do as president apart from laying the wreath at the War Memorial and presiding over AGMs. I'd enjoyed my term but I became quite disabled physically so thought it best to retire.

Geoff Lewis

Scouts/Boys' Brigade

Bob-a-Job
As a Wolf Cub I did 'bob-a-job' during the Easter holidays, which usually meant helping with the spring cleaning. I belonged to the 3rd Cranham Troop of the Boy Scouts, which was run by Mr Sorrell and his wife who lived in Isis Drive, and based at a hut next to St Luke's Church.

The Boys' Brigade was much more prominent. I remember seeing their church parades going down to the Baptist church. The Baptist church was a major force on the estate in the late 1950s, even with people who had never been Baptists flocking to it. St Luke's had a good start with the Revd Jones, who cycled round the estate and was very popular, but the congregation declined when he was replaced by the Revd Hart.

When I was in the Scouts we went to the off-sales, as it was quaintly called, at the Golden Crane. It was the only place on the estate that could sell alcohol due to a restrictive covenant placed on the land by the former owners, Charringtons the brewers. We bought crisps and soft drinks such as bitter lemon. The door and serving counter were made of heavy oak and I remember the yeasty smell of spilt beer.

Peter Morris

The Drums
I was in the Boys' Brigade, which helped me to socialise because working on a farm can be isolating. Before I left school I was in the Boys' Brigade in South Ockendon and finished up as bandmaster because I played the drums.

Reflections

Bert Bonnett with the Boys' Brigade, *c.* 1960.

I was about thirteen when I joined the Boys' Brigade, and when I left it in my thirties I was an officer. Boys learn discipline and the like when they join groups like the Boys' Brigade and the Scouts. I think they miss out these days as not many seem to join organisations like that. Baden Powell was involved with the Boys' Brigade before he took up with the Scouts.

Bert Bonnett

The Bugle
I belonged to the Scouts and we met in the grounds of St Laurence Church. There were some old buildings which were converted into patrol houses behind what I think were some old stables. There were six patrols and they had a Cub troop too, but they'd been full when I tried to join, so I had to go to the Boys' Brigade which met in the Baptist church in Springfield Gardens. When I was in the Scouts I played the bugle and we had church parade once a month.

Alex Duffey

Working in the Convent Grounds

One of my father's jobs was to look after the gardens at the convent and I'd accompany him during school holidays and at weekends. To a child's mind the grounds were massive. There were yew trees which must have been there for years as they were huge with branches as thick as the trunks on a normal tree. They began some 20ft up the trunk before branching out like the hand of God. There must have been a variety of trees because in the autumn there'd be plenty of conkers lying on the ground. The orchard was wonderful – there always seemed to be apples lying on the floor. I remember old sheds with corroded machinery and bits of rusty tools inside, and it was fun to lumber around in there. The potting shed was a haven for me as sometimes the schoolgirls used to gather in groups to ask me questions about myself, which I found embarrassing at the time, but they were very nice girls.

The grass was also beautifully maintained and I recall the grounds as always being bathed in sunshine; there seemed to be no winter. And yet, I can remember those wonderful trees in autumn, when they shed their leaves. Millions of them, and I had to sweep them up. The grounds were fantastic and when we took a break for a meal we'd use the servants' entrance into the kitchen. We'd be looked after by Sister Dorothy, who was a wonderful person. She was kind and loving but also strict and she could be dogmatic, preferring to do things her own way. She was one of those people with a presence, who could dominate a room.

The kitchen itself was quite basic and always immaculate, with a proper wooden kitchen table where Sister Dorothy used to do her chopping and prepare the vegetables. There wasn't a great deal in the kitchen, but I remember the butler sink and the room itself as being big and cold. Even the floor was cold. Outside the kitchen there was a small room where we had our meals. It only had a table and two benches, and salt and pepper pots were always on the table, plus a bowl of sugar.

It was Sister Dorothy's job to cook and she always seemed to be in the kitchen. When breakfast was finished she started preparing lunch and when that was over she started on dinner. She made the most fantastic Irish stew and even today I can remember it – the spoon would stand up in the white bowl. Sister Dorothy always wore a different coloured tunic to everybody else. Hers was blue whereas the other nuns wore black, and she always wore an apron. She was very fond of my father. They sort of took to each other and she became part of our family. I think when Pop passed over she thought we'd forget her but we continued to visit, although whether she was as close to us as she was to Pop I'm not sure. She was always such a good host, giving us tea and biscuits. When she grew old it was surprising how the other nuns fussed around and looked after her. It was wonderful to see because she'd been cooking for other people all her life and now they were looking after her.

The chapel, which was inside the house, was beautiful and peaceful. If you believe in God you'd be convinced He was there. Novices would come over from Ireland to stay with the nuns and go back home during school holidays – they were wonderful young girls. The nuns didn't dress the way they do now. They used to wear habits in those days and you recognised them as nuns. I remember them pulling my hair to one side to inspect my ears to see if I'd washed them.

Kevin Mallon

Other local titles published by The History Press

Canvey Island Revisited
GEOFF BARSBY

Sitting just off the Essex coast and surrounded by water on all sides, Canvey Island's location has contributed to its intriguing past. All over there is evidence of its history, such as the pillboxes built during the Second World War. Following on from the first two collections of archive images, this new volume revisits the Canvey Island of yesteryear with the use of 200 fascinating photographs and postcards, and is an important pictorial history that will be of interest to all those who have ever lived in the area.

978 0 7524 3984 6

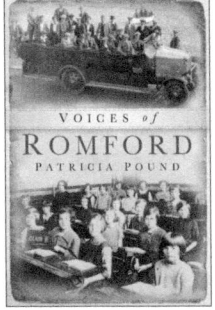

Voices of Romford
PAT POUND

This collection of shared personal memories of Romford gives a fascinating insight into experiences in the twentieth century. This volume provides recollections of how they lived through schooldays, enjoyed play, working life, sport, entertainment, and how the world wars affected families. The personal reminiscences are complimented by over 100 photographs from the participants' private collections and illustrate features of the town's past.

978 0 7524 4758 2

Rainham and Wennington Memories
CECILIA PYKE

The villages of Rainham and Wennington are closely linked, with the area having been shaped into the place it is today by the people, some of whose experiences and reminiscences are recorded here. This book brings together the personal memories of people who have lived and worked here, vividly recalling childhood and working life, shops and entertainment, and the war years. The many absorbing stories are complemented by around 100 photographs.

978 0 7524 3671 5

Basildon Our Heritage
FRANCES CLAMP

Basildon was one of the New Towns created after the Second World War to deal with some of the housing problems after years of conflict. Yet people have lived in the area throughout recorded history. The Basildon Heritage Project worked with children from five local primary schools who were introduced to digital cameras and used their new skills in helping to establish the Basildon Heritage Trail. The children are the future of the town and their involvement has made them aware of their valuable heritage.

978 0 7524 4551 9

If you are interested in purchasing other books published by The History Press, or in case you have difficulty finding any History Press books in your local bookshop, you can also place orders directly through our website

www.thehistorypress.co.uk